Contents

We Went to the **Underground City of Nightmares**
1

An **Elder God** Was **Revived**
27

We Went to an **Improved Apple** Exhibition
59

We Went to a **Cat Café**
87

We Thought About This Year's
Witch's House Café
125

We Opened the
Witch's House Café Again
143

BONUS

We Spent a Day Making Curry and Chaos Ensued
175

BONUS

The Family Planned a Surprise for Me
217

Story by Kisetsu Morita   Illustration by Benio

She slaughtered slimes for 300 years...

©Benio

I've Been Killing SLIMES for 300 Years and Maxed Out My Level 14

Kisetsu Morita

Illustration by Benio

Yen On

NEW YORK

I've Been Killing SLIMES for 300 Years and Maxed Out My Level 14

KISETSU MORITA

Translation by Jasmine Bernhardt
Cover art by Benio

This book is a work of fiction. Names, characters, places, and incidents are the product of the author's imagination or are used fictitiously. Any resemblance to actual events, locales, or persons, living or dead, is coincidental.

SLIME TAOSHITE SANBYAKUNEN, SHIRANAIUCHINI LEVEL MAX NI NATTEMASHITA vol. 14
Copyright © 2020 Kisetsu Morita
Illustrations copyright © 2020 Benio
All rights reserved.
Original Japanese edition published in 2020 by SB Creative Corp.

This English edition is published by arrangement with SB Creative Corp., Tokyo in care of Tuttle-Mori Agency, Inc., Tokyo.

English translation © 2024 by Yen Press, LLC

Yen Press, LLC supports the right to free expression and the value of copyright. The purpose of copyright is to encourage writers and artists to produce the creative works that enrich our culture.

The scanning, uploading, and distribution of this book without permission is a theft of the author's intellectual property. If you would like permission to use material from the book (other than for review purposes), please contact the publisher. Thank you for your support of the author's rights.

Yen On
150 West 30th Street, 19th Floor
New York, NY 10001

Visit us at yenpress.com
facebook.com/yenpress
twitter.com/yenpress
yenpress.tumblr.com
instagram.com/yenpress

First Yen On Edition: January 2024
Edited by Yen On Editorial: Emma McClain, Anna Powers
Designed by Yen Press Design: Liz Parlett, Wendy Chan

Yen On is an imprint of Yen Press, LLC.
The Yen On name and logo are trademarks of Yen Press, LLC.

The publisher is not responsible for websites (or their content) that are not owned by the publisher.

Library of Congress Cataloging-in-Publication Data
Names: Morita, Kisetsu, author. | Benio, illustrator. | Engel, Taylor, translator. | Bernhardt, Jasmine, translator
Title: I've been killing slimes for 300 years and maxed out my level / Kisetsu Morita; illustration by Benio.
Other titles: Slime taoshite sanbyakunen, shiranaiuchini level max ni nattemashita. English |
I have been killing slimes for 300 years
Description: First Yen On edition. | New York: Yen On, 2018— |
v. 1–2, 6: translation by Taylor Engel. | v. 3–14: translation by Jasmine Bernhardt.
Identifiers: LCCN 2017059843 | ISBN 9780316448277 (v. 1: pbk.) | ISBN 9780316448291 (v. 2: pbk.) |
ISBN 9781975329310 (v. 3: pbk.) | ISBN 9781975382636 (v. 4: pbk.) | ISBN 9781975382650 (v. 5: pbk.) |
ISBN 9781975382674 (v. 6: pbk.) | ISBN 9781975312916 (v. 7: pbk.) | ISBN 9781975314811 (v. 8: pbk.) |
ISBN 9781975318338 (v. 9: pbk.) | ISBN 9781975318352 (v. 10: pbk.) | ISBN 9781975339791 (v. 11: pbk.) |
ISBN 9781975340573 (v. 12: pbk.) | ISBN 9781975340551 (v. 13: pbk.) | ISBN 9781975340575 (v. 14: pbk.)
Subjects: CYAC: Reincarnation—Fiction. | Witches—Fiction.
Classification: LCC PZ7.1.M6725 Iv 2018 | DDC [Fic]—dc23
LC record available at https://lccn.loc.gov/2017059843

ISBNs: 978-1-9753-4057-5 (paperback)
978-1-9753-4058-2 (ebook)

1 3 5 7 9 10 8 6 4 2

LBK

Printed in the United States of America

AZUSA AIZAWA

The protagonist. Commonly known as the Witch of the Highlands. A girl (?) who was reincarnated as an immortal witch with the appearance of a seventeen-year-old. Before she knew what was happening, she'd become the strongest being in the world. Although she's had some rough times, it has ultimately given her a family, and she's delighted about it.

"PERSEVERANCE EQUALS POWER. I ONLY DO THINGS I CAN STICK WITH!"

BEELZEBUB

A high-ranking demon known as the Lord of the Flies and the demons' minister of agriculture. She treats Falfa and Shalsha as her own nieces and frequently shuttles between the demon realm and the house in the highlands. She's also Azusa's reliable "big sister" surrogate.

"MY NAME IS BEELZEBUB, AGRICULTURAL MINISTER OF THE DEMON REALM!"

FALFA AND SHALSHA

Spirit sisters born from a conglomeration of slime souls. Falfa, the older sister, is a carefree girl who's honest about her own feelings. Shalsha, the younger sister, is considerate and attentive to others. They both love their mother, Azusa.

LAIKA AND FLATORTE

Red and blue dragon-girls who live in the house in the highlands. Laika is Azusa's apprentice and a good, hardworking girl. Flatorte is a cheerful, energetic girl who obeys what Azusa says. They tend to compete with each other as fellow dragons.

HALKARA

A young elf woman and Azusa's apprentice. She is an upstanding CEO who runs a company using her knowledge of mushrooms, but in the house in the highlands, she's known for her knack for screwing up.

ROSALIE

A ghost girl and resident of the house in the highlands. She's devoted to Azusa, who didn't shy away from her as a ghost and instead reached out to her. She can go through walls but can't touch people. She can also possess others.

SANDRA

A mandragora girl. After growing for three hundred years, she gained sentience and the ability to move around. She is a literal plant and lives in the vegetable garden in the house in the highlands. She's often stubborn and puts up a front, but she also craves the company of others.

PECORA
(PROVATO PECORA ARIÉS)

The Demon King. A girl with a devilish temperament who loves to use her power and influence to bewilder her subordinates and Azusa. She actually has a masochistic desire to be subordinate to someone stronger than she is, and she adores Azusa.

GOODLY GODLY GODNESS

The very being who reincarnated Azusa into this world. An upbeat and affable but careless goddess who fits perfectly in this world. She has a soft spot for women and tends to make lenient decisions.

THE GODDESS NINTAN

A goddess long worshipped in this world. She is a troublesome one, always looking down on others and turning people she doesn't like into frogs, but after losing a fight to a human (Azusa, who broke the level cap), she softened a bit.

OST ANDE

The reaper of this world. She only does the bare minimum required for her position and spends her free time writing and submitting novels. She has never been very adept at communication, which worries Nintan. After Nintan summoned Azusa and Godly Godness to have tea with her, they became conversation partners.

MUUM MUUM

Nickname: Muu. Sovereign of the ghosts' kingdom of the dead, as well as the ruler of an ancient civilization that is now destroyed. Though she had holed herself up after growing fed up with her wet-blanket people (the poltergeists), she made a return to society (?) after coming into contact with Azusa and Rosalie. She has an accent and loves banter.

NAHNA NAHNA

Chief maid and minister of the dead kingdom. Minds Muu as her adviser and caretaker. She is earnest and capable, but she has a sharp wit and loves making others squirm. Once she finds Muu's and Azusa's weaknesses and pet peeves, she annoys them indirectly.

MISJANTIE

A pine spirit. Though she was once revered as the being who mediated marriages, the practice has recently fallen out of use, and she's losing her cool over it. After meeting Azusa and the others, she set up a temple (branch) in Flatta.

WE WENT TO THE UNDERGROUND CITY OF NIGHTMARES

That day, the sky was ominous from the moment we woke up.

Thunder rumbled in the clouds.

"Halkara, I'm not letting you fly to work today. We might get struck by lightning," Flatorte said while looking out the window during breakfast.

Dragons were a big target, after all.

"I could go through the clouds and fly above them, but Nascúte is way too close for that. And the clouds themselves would be dangerous."

"Ahhh, you're right. Even a creature as huge as you wouldn't be able to survive a lightning strike," Halkara mused.

"Hey, don't get the wrong idea, Halkara. I, the great Flatorte, am not so weak that I'd fall to one measly little lightning strike. I've been struck five times in one day before, and I walked it off."

Laika was staring dully at Flatorte—I had a feeling not even dragons typically flew on days with weather like this…

"But if lightning *did* strike me, you'd probably die on my back, Halkara. And I don't think I'd like that."

"Eep… I think I'll walk to work…"

Good choice. If anything, she should probably stay home until the storm clouds go.

I gazed out the window.

"The weather here in the highlands is usually calm, but there sure is a lot of thunder out there today…"

Sometimes, I could even see a flash of lightning in the distance.

"It is unusual to see stormy weather at this time of year in Nanterre. I do not think I ever experienced such awful weather at Mount Rokko, either."

"I thought you might agree, Laika. It gets cold sometimes, but it's easy living besides that."

Goodly Godly Godness had chosen this place for me when I reincarnated as a witch, after all, so it couldn't be an awful place to live.

"Mmm. Big Sis? I sense something."

Rosalie was floating near the ceiling, and—

—part of her hair was sticking straight up, like she'd just gotten out of bed!

"I think this is a bad sign," she said.

"Rosalie, was your hair able to detect weird magic before…?"

The longer I looked at it, the more it reminded me of an antenna.

"I think it means that something major is going to happen. This might be a first; I don't remember it ever happening before."

"Huh. Are you sure it isn't some kind of retcon…?" I asked. "This didn't happen when we first visited Muu, remember?"

Muu had incredible spirit power. And while I'd never seen it for myself, I was sure Nahna Nahna's strength was impressive, too.

"And we know the demon king and multiple gods. There really isn't much left that can outclass them."

"You are right. But if we put them all together, it would mean that whatever we are facing is even more dangerous—"

"Nah. That's way too far-fetched!"

But Rosalie's intuition was right. The dark and stormy clouds passed, and the sky grew light again. There, out the window, I spotted something flying toward us.

It was a wyvern. And it seemed to be headed straight for the house in the highlands.

Not much later, Fatla came through the door.

"Sorry for stopping by so early, but Miss Azusa is needed immediately." Fatla was calm, as she usually was, but there was a hint of panic in her voice. "We will reward your services with a lecturer's fee afterward."

"Hold your horses. Can't you at least tell me why I have to go first?"

"The reasons are yet unclear. I am hoping it is a false alarm, however…"

Fatla paused and took a breath. I'd never seen her so upset before.

I put some tea on to boil. Whatever was the matter, it couldn't be too urgent for tea.

The whole family naturally sharpened their ears to listen. Even Sandra, who had been in the garden, came inside to hear.

"Not long ago, the dryad sage Miyu-miyu Kuzzoco came to visit the Smart Slime, and they have been conducting research together ever since."

"Oh, Miyu, the world's third-hardest sage to meet."

Miyu the dryad sage lived on Outofreach Island, which, as the name suggested, was very hard to reach due to ocean currents. Though Miyu was something of a valley girl, she was very smart.

"It's easy to leave the island, though. All you have to do is get caught in a current, and you're automatically sent straight to the shore."

"It is as you say. I hear it is very easy to reach the harbor cities on the mainland. She arrived on a small boat, and I then took her to Vanzeld Castle via wyvern."

An image of Smarsly and Miyu debating endlessly crossed my mind.

"I'm really glad Smarsly has a friend it can better itself with."

"Indeed. The Smart Slime and Miyu-miyu Kuzzoco have been having plenty of delightful conversations. However…"

Fatla paused to loudly sip at her tea. Her expression was dark, even for someone as stern as she was.

"They were studying an ancient clay tablet discovered underground in demon territory when they learned that something rather terrible was written on it…"

Now, there's something I haven't heard of yet, I thought just as Shalsha opened a book and began to explain.

"Ancient clay tablets are historic records hidden underground in the demon lands and written in a strange language. Even the demons do not know what exactly they are."

I'd never heard of anything like that before.

"Is that true?" I asked. "I was under the impression that demon civilization has continued unbroken for ages. I didn't think there were other cultures in your territory…"

"As you say," continued Shalsha, "there are some demons who insist the tablets were simply left by ancient demons who spoke a different language. But they have yet to be decoded, so it has long remained a mystery."

How long ago were we talking about here? My three hundred years of life was probably a blip compared to demon history.

"Miss Fatla? What was written on the tablet?"

Falfa was curious, too. I guess if someone told me they'd learned the secrets of an ancient civilization, I'd be pretty interested.

"I am not entirely sure of the details myself," she said. "But…apparently, if a certain seal is broken, very bad things will happen. Very, very bad things."

I wasn't sure what she meant by that—just that it was very bad.

"So you want me to go with you to make sure the seal stays shut? Is that what you mean?"

I tried to interpret the reason for Fatla's visit in my own words.

"No. There will not be a problem if the seal remains intact. We need you in case the seal is broken and something emerges."

"And you're paying me a *lecturer's fee* for that?!"

That had to be illegal… Could she at least be a little less cryptic…?

"I am sorry. We don't have a budget allocated for the reawakening of ancient horrors... Once we have a grasp on the full picture, we will compensate you accordingly."

I felt like I was seeing Fatla act like a bureaucrat for the first time in a while.

I shot up from my chair.

"I'm ready to go whenever you are."

I didn't particularly *want* to go, but this didn't sound like something I could ignore. And I couldn't just sit around relaxing in the house in the highlands after hearing all that... Besides, if things got out of hand, there was a very good chance they'd come and ask for my help again...

"Thank you so much." Fatla smiled at last. "I hope the seal remains unbroken. However..."

"Careful, don't jinx it!"

Now it was *definitely* going to break.

I sincerely hoped Fatla was just being a worrywart...

The only family members headed to Vanzeld Castle were Laika, Flatorte, and I.

We shot up straight through a break in the clouds and flew over them.

I rode on Laika's back, and Fatla rode on Flatorte. It was a lot quicker than going back on the wyvern.

This was considerably shadier than anything else we'd done so far, so I didn't want to bring the girls and Halkara along. Since I didn't know what we would be up against, either, I had Rosalie stay at home, too.

"Still, I am surprised there are civilizations so old that even the demons don't know about them."

Laika's loud voice was audible despite how fast we were moving.

"Not *that* weird," said Flatorte. "The demons didn't know about the country of ghosts, remember? There's bound to be a few more they missed."

As she said, the demons hadn't been involved with the Thursa Thursa Kingdom.

"Miss Muu's civilization lies far beyond the demon lands' borders," Laika pointed out. "But the tablet was buried in demon territory. I find it surprising that demons do not know about the civilization right beneath their noses."

"That's true," I said. "I thought the demons had *always* lived there, like you, Laika. But…if you think about it logically, I guess that isn't so. There had to be a beginning, huh?"

I'd never studied demon history thoroughly, but even the demons must have had their own version of a Paleolithic era and "Unga bunga" ancestors.

Unless they'd all suddenly arrived from another world, they couldn't have built a great structure like Vanzeld Castle on day one.

"We don't know how far back that was, and their history goes much deeper than that of the human kingdom, but the demons must have had a primitive age, too. So does that mean the tablet is from a civilization even older than that, and something from that previous era is going to reawaken?" I asked, turning to Fatla where she sat on Flatorte's back.

"I believe so," she replied. "To be honest, I thought it mere myth."

Ancient history probably had nothing to do with her day-to-day life, so it made sense she didn't know much. The only people who would know this kind of info would be those specifically interested in the subject.

"I do not know enough to give you any details. You will have to listen to what the Smart Slime and the dryad Miyu-miyu Kuzzoco have to say. I hope it turns out we were all worried for nothing…"

"I, the great Flatorte, want to fight with some crazy-big thing I've never heard of before!"

Not the time, Flatorte!

But if her goal was to test her strength, then a situation as exciting as this would be hard to pass up. That said, there was no guarantee the "bad" thing in question was a powerful enemy. All we had at this point was conjecture.

So much of this was yet to be determined, and that made me even more nervous as we hurried toward Vanzeld Castle.

As I was pelted by wind—less a comfortable cool and more a chilling cold—an idea hit me.

Now that I thought about it, Godly Godness or Nintan might know something. They were deities, after all. They *had* to know what had come before the demons.

But I had no way of reaching them at the moment.

I tried thinking out loud in my mind, *Goddess, can you hear me?* But there was no response. Of course.

They, on the other hand, could appear out of the blue in my dreams. I found this a little unfair, but it was disrespectful of me as a mortal to want to stand on equal ground with gods, so I let it go.

...But thinking about it another way—if the situation was way worse than we thought, maybe the gods were already trying to stop it...

I shook my head.

What did I mean, trying? Nothing could defeat a god. Only another entity of equal power would stand a chance.

"I wanna fight a god!" Flatorte shouted.

I wished I could take things as easily as she did!

We arrived safely and were brought into a room deep in Vanzeld Castle where classified information was handled.

Inside stood Miyu and Smarsly engaged in a heated back-and-forth.

To be more precise, Smarsly couldn't talk, so it was hopping around furiously on its cloth keyboard to form words. Still, I could tell they were having some kind of discussion.

"Omigooosh! Is that Azusa and the gang?! Omigosh, things are like, super, suuuper crazy right now! The craziest craziness I've ever seen!"

Hearing her use the word *crazy* so many times made the situation sound a lot less serious than it probably was.

"Miyu, you have to be more specific," I said. "What's happening?"

"It's sooo *crazy* underground in the demon territory right now. Like, it actually cracks me up."

"You have to be *specific*! And this isn't funny! There is nothing to laugh about!"

I knew, logically, that she was a sage, but she was so smart that it was difficult to communicate with her.

Smarsly hopped over its keyboard cloth, spelling out a word: "Danger."

This, too, was frustratingly vague. But—

"…Right. Smarsly would get tired explaining everything to us, so I guess we'll have to ask Miyu…"

But just then, the door opened, and two familiar faces walked in—Beelzebub and Pecora.

"Things are getting rather out of hand, Elder Sister~"

The look on Pecora's face said she wasn't worried in the slightest, however. It'd be nice if that meant there really was no cause for worry, but Beelzebub was scowling.

"What do we know right now?" I asked. "I don't care who it is. Just—one of you—tell me what's happening."

"Of course," Beelzebub replied. "When Miyu arrived, she wished to amuse herself and began examining an ancient clay tablet we have been unable to decipher as idle amusement."

"She was doing it for fun…?"

"Both Smarsly and Miyu are sages, yes? I thought they might be able to read these clay tablets we've had lying around undeciphered for years, so I brought them out for fun. I thought it'd be worth it if they even managed one word."

The situation didn't call for mincing words, but wasn't she being a little too honest?

"But they learned something—if I may borrow Miyu's wording—*crazy*."

"Please don't."

We were getting nowhere. I just wanted someone to tell me what the problem was.

"The following was written on the tablet: *Should our god be freed, we will rule these lands far and wide.*"

"A god?!" I exclaimed. "And it's been sealed away all this time, I bet..."

That might indeed cause something truly terrible to happen.

"For the time being," Pecora began, "we have decided to call this sealed entity an elder god—something entirely different from the sort of god we demons worship. Additionally, the clay tablets seem to have been made by unknown intelligent beings. Whoever created them is unlike modern demons, the humans' ancestors, and of course the elves' and dwarves' ancestors, too~"

There was a bundle of paper in Pecora's hands—probably a report on the investigation.

"If that's true," I said, "then we need to make sure the seal stays intact."

"Yeeeaaah! Time to fight an elder god!" shouted Flatorte.

But that was risky... Even I couldn't handle something like that.

"Aye, that was the intention. However..."

Beelzebub and Pecora exchanged glances.

"We need to hurry. Otherwise, the seal might undo itself! ♪" Pecora said shyly, then gripped my hands. "That's why I'd like to ask you to take a look at the seal, Elder Sister. This may be the greatest danger demonkind—no, the world itself has ever experienced~ Oh gosh, look at me! Taking advantage of the situation to hold your hand!"

"You don't sound too upset, but…we're in trouble, correct?"

It wasn't possible the problem had already been solved, right? Pecora loved pulling stunts like that…

"Yes," she replied. "It's a serious matter to face a god~"

"Yeah, totally!" Miyu piped up. "It's the *craziest craziness* I've ever seen!"

"Things are *crazy*, Azusa," Beelzebub added. "You must help us."

"Man," Flatorte said. "Imagine how fun it'd be if the god or whatever was *crazy* strong!"

"Okay, none of you are allowed to say 'crazy' until—until all this is over!"

I didn't know what was happening anymore. This had to be the most times I'd heard the word *crazy* in a day.

"Lady Azusa…," said Laika. "The word *crazy* has stopped sounding like a real word anymore… All I can hear is a combination of 'cuh,' 'ray,' and 'zee'…"

She was tired of this, too. It appeared she was experiencing semantic satiation.

"You think this is all pretty *crazy*, too, don't you, Laika?"

"Oh, Lady Azusa, you just said it yourself…"

"………You're right."

I guess my words were being influenced by the people around me, too…

"Okay, Beelzebub," I said. "Do you know where this seal is? I heard it's underground, but are we talking right beneath Vanzeld Castle again?"

That was the first thing that came to mind. The area beneath the castle was like a giant maze. In that respect, it was exactly the kind of place a demon king would call home.

"Not the castle, no," Beelzebub replied. "It's probably in the area where the tablet was discovered. 'Tis reasonable to believe that the seal would be around there as well."

"I guess you're right."

It was a safe bet to assume the ominous clay tablet about the revival of an elder god had been located near its subject.

"So we just need to go to the place it was found. I can leave right now."

"...You're rather motivated today, aren't you?" Beelzebub noted.

Well, I was! Don't take the wind out of my sails!

"You're the ones who dragged me into this... I may not know much about what's going on, but it sounds like the whole world is dangerous. I can't exactly look the other way, whether I want to get involved or not..."

"It is as Lady Azusa says," Laika added. "For what reason have we refined our strength, if not to shine in situations like this?"

Laika was earnest, as always. Her parents must be proud.

Beelzebub nodded slowly. "Very well. Then we shall move before the sun sets."

After splitting into groups to ride wyverns, we made our way to our destination.

The two dragons were also on wyverns so that they could recover the energy they'd spent getting to the demon lands. Smarsly and Miyu had come along, too. Miyu was holding Smarsly.

She had brought a bag with her, but it was stuffed full of potatoes to help her replenish her mana. Dryads had to stay charged, otherwise things would get "crazy" (and no, I'm not really sure what that means), so whenever they traveled any distance, they needed to bring along what was essentially a mobile battery.

"Are you sure Smarsly and Miyu should be joining us?"

They didn't seem like fighting types, so I was worried.

"It's not like we're in a battle at the moment," Miyu replied. "And we might find new tablets, which could give us more info. We have to chase the latest trends, otherwise our research will be worthless!"

Was research like fashion? Did it have trends?

But Miyu was right, in a way—research from five hundred years ago was outdated by today's standards and not very useful.

"When you're researching a trend, you *have* to find the source. We know that wherever this tablet came from is absolutely cuh-rayzee, so we gotta go there and find out how crazy it really is!"

"Researching a trend..."

This talk reminded me of going to Harajuku or Daikanyama. When I was in high school, I would go to Harajuku and walk around eating sweets. I didn't seek out the latest trends, but I did act like a classic high school girl.

"If I may add to what Dryad Miyu just said," Beelzebub interjected. She was sitting in front of me on the same wyvern. "The seal is not undone, nor is the locale a war zone. Thus, it is perfectly acceptable for you to treat this as a sightseeing tour to a city out in the middle of nowhere."

"Right. Even if the seal mentioned on the tablet is real, if nothing is happening, it must still be functioning as intended."

"Precisely."

But what would a rural city in the demon lands be like?

The wyverns landed before a massive shrine.

The problem was...there was nothing *but* the shrine.

The surrounding area was all wasteland. I couldn't spot anything remotely resembling a house. There weren't even any trees. It was just a shrine standing in the middle of nowhere.

"What now? You call this a rural city? Something's not right..."

Flatorte was already wandering around the outside of the shrine, muttering, "They don't even sell food. This place sucks."

"Oh, maybe it's a huge shrine, and the rest is just buried? That can happen to ancient cities in the desert. But that would make it a ruin, so I still don't think you can call it a rural city."

"Azusa," Beelzebub said. "What are you talking about? This is a station at best."

Clearly, we were not on the same page.

Fatla was the first to enter the shrine. Then Pecora, then Beelzebub. I had no choice but to follow.

Inside, the shrine was rather spacious, with a sudden slope. And that slope was headed down into the earth.

"What is this...?" Laika had never seen anything like it before, and she was staring, wide-eyed.

The ceiling was high, but there was nothing filling the space. It was totally open. The slope was the only thing inside.

"This station takes us to the underground city of Yostos. This is the only way one may enter Yostos," Beelzebub said, breezing right past the phrase *underground city*.

"You have cities underground?! I didn't know about this! You should've told me!"

"Oh, 'tis common knowledge among us, so I suppose I forgot..."

The demon world was much deeper than I thought—*literally*.

"Elder Sister," Pecora piped up. "There are some demons who do not handle sunlight well. They make their cities underground and live there."

"Demons are on a whole other level... Wait, does that mean the underground city is in total darkness?"

"Oh, no, don't worry about that. This city is for people who simply cannot handle sunlight. They are fine with other types of light. I think it might even be brighter than the surface!"

"So we're not going to be stumbling around blind. But how are we supposed to get undergr—?"

The rest of my sentence was drowned out by the sound of massive footsteps. Huge mole-like demons appeared from what was probably the shrine guardroom. The moles were pulling several linked mine carts behind them.

"We'll be getting on the King Mole. Even those who can fly have difficulty diving straight down into the earth, so we typically travel on these."

"Yet another new vehicle, I see..."

We all got on the mine carts.

Flatorte and I took the cart at the very front. The demons all seemed to gather toward the back.

A metal gate then slowly lifted open. Beyond the gate was an abyss of inky blackness. There probably weren't any lights beyond this point.

"Ooh... I don't...I don't know if I like this..." Laika grabbed at my back, probably unconsciously.

"I doubt the city itself is in total darkness, so just hang in there for a bit, okay, Laika?"

"Lady Azusa, please forgive me if I get scared and let some fire out..."

"Please try to keep it in, okay?"

I didn't want to be made into roasted Azusa.

The mine carts reminded me of amusement park rides. I didn't think any went straight down like this, though. Hm, now that I thought about it, I did notice some handrails inside the carts. What could those be for?

"Sheesh, you little crybaby, Laika," said Flatorte. "It's just dark. If that scares you, you must be scared every night when you go to sleep!"

It seemed Flatorte had some immunity to the horrors of the dark. She was being quite logical about all this. Though in her case, it was probably less that she was hard to scare and more that she was simply not thinking very deeply about it.

"I can't help it... I do not know where my enemy is in the dark, and it puts me at a disadvantage. It is normal to be afraid of such a prospect..." Meanwhile, Laika was clinging to my back.

"Hah. You always talk a big game, but all it takes is a little dark—"

The mine carts suddenly lurched downward.

"Gah! I just bit my tongue!"

Flatorte's scream echoed off the earthen walls.

The King Mole had begun to rush down the slope, which was probably where the lurch came from.

With that, the mine carts raced straight into the darkness!

I couldn't see *anything*.

I could only feel the jostling of the mine carts.

Now I got why there were handrails... Shouldn't the demons have warned me about this?! It was my first time, after all.

"Eek! I'm so scared! Lady Azusa, this is terrifying!" Laika's screams were coming from right behind me.

"I know! This is basically a roller coaster!"

It was hard to tell in the dark, but I was sure the moles were running pretty fast. There were even times when it felt like we were falling straight down. Anyone who hates this stuff should steer clear of this mode of transport... It reminded me of those rides where you were blindfolded and then dropped from way up high...

"Hey!" shouted Beelzebub. "You'll bite your tongue if you speak! Do not open your mouth!"

"You should've told me that before! You always wait until after the fact! Like with the shrine-station!"

"...'Tis common knowledge for a demon, so I forgot."

I'm not a demon, you know. Please, just explain things.

"Gosh, it is nice to take a ride in these every once in a while, isn't it~?"

"Aaaah-ha-ha-ha-ha-ha! This is sooo fun! It's sooo funny! Like, *super* funny! ♪ I'm getting sooo hyped right now!"

I could hear Pecora and Miyu laughing... They really were treating this like an amusement park...

At last, it didn't feel like we were falling anymore.

Finally, we'd made it—

—except an instant later it felt like we were whipping around a tight corner.

"Waaaaaaah! Now whaaaaaat?!" Laika exclaimed.

"It's moving like a roller coasteeeeeer!" I screamed.

"We call this Hell's Spiral. Do not let go," Beelzebub warned. "If you are thrown from the cart, it will be a pain finding and rescuing you in the dark."

"Don't tell me that nooooow!"

"Omigosh! This is crazy! This is *so* crazy! I'm cracking up! Ooomigosh! This is so crazy!"

Miyu had gone full Valley girl...

"Miss Miyu is a genuine sage... She sees everything from a distance and feels no fear... I still have a long way to go..."

Laika, you are giving her way too much credit...

"Whoa! Ha-ha, omigosh, I almost dropped Smarsly!"

"Please, hold on to it tightly!" I shouted. "Keep a death grip on it!"

Smarsly was already black; if it fell into the darkness, who knows how long the search would take...

"Oh! It's the Spiral-After-Spiral next~ Be careful, everyone~!"

Right after Pecora said that, I felt my body jerk in an uncomfortable direction...

I really wished they'd told us all this before we started, but if I'd asked for too many details, Laika probably would've been too scared to get on...

Despite going through full vertical circuit on the way, we eventually arrived at the station for the underground city of Yostos. It was properly lit, so we were able to see all right. The building itself was not too different from the one aboveground.

"Phew... We finally made it... That went on forever...," I said.

"It did...," Laika agreed. "It felt as though I was having a nightmare from which I would never awaken..."

We were both mentally exhausted.

"It was so nice and cool. Being underground is really comfortable."

Flatorte sounded as carefree as ever. I wished I could be as relaxed as her. Was there any reason the route had done a full loop?

"'Tis not a long ride at all. It took scarcely ten minutes. The King Mole goes quite fast, you see."

"No, Beelzebub, I mean it felt like it would never end. How much time it actually took isn't the problem..."

All the demons seemed unfazed, as though they were used to such things. Maybe this was just a cultural difference...

"Omigosh, that was the *best*! I got so craaaazy excited! I totally wanna go again!"

"We're not here to play, Miyu! You do realize we came all this way for a very serious reason, right?"

However, once we exited the station, I immediately wanted to eat my words.

The underground city was filled to the brim with color and joy.

There were signs in the shape of candy and food, and the walls were painted with murals of cats, dogs, and ducks. The shops were awfully vibrant, and it felt totally different from the town around Vanzeld Castle. Cheerful music poured out from every kind of establishment.

What's more, the demons walking around were wearing fake bunny ears.

And despite how far underground we were—or rather, because of it—the place was full of light magic.

I knew this atmosphere—

"This is just like the Kingdom of Dreams!"

"Oh-ho. It seems you *have* heard a thing or two about this place," Beelzebub said. "You are close, but it would be more accurate to call it the Nightmare City. Many nightmares live here, you see."

So I was right about the rest of it...

"Most nightmares like to live among frivolity. Apparently, it allows for more variation in dreams."

"So that's why it's like a theme park…"

"'Tis indeed lively, yes. Some of the residents have many eyes, others have big eyes—they do not like the sun, so they live here. I find it hard to relax in this atmosphere, so I am not particularly fond of it."

Behind Beelzebub passed a little band all playing trumpets. It *was* loud—not a place I could see her enjoying.

"So where in this underground city are we supposed to go…?"

If someone here told me an evil god's seal was on the verge of breaking, I would almost assume they were telling me about a new ride.

"We can go to the place where the tablet was discovered," Beelzebub offered. "As you can see, the area around the King Mole has been highly developed. We shall make our way to a place more remo— And why are some of us already treating this like a field trip?"

Both Flatorte and Miyu had bunny ears on.

"Some guy who passed by gave them to us. The people here are kinda funny."

"They're sooo nice! Omigosh, I think I love this place."

It really was just like an amusement park… I couldn't believe the demons had been hiding such a bizarre place this whole time.

Once the situation was resolved, I thought I might bring the kids here. They'd probably have a lot of fun. In fact, it was *so* much like an amusement park that I found it strange Beelzebub hadn't already tried to bring them…

Maybe theme parks just weren't a thing in her mind, and that was why she could only see it as a loud, overbearing city.

I couldn't be sure, but I got the feeling she'd always had a somewhat distorted view of the world, even as a kid. I found it impossible to picture baby Beelzebub enjoying herself at an amusement park.

"Hey, Azusa," called Beelzebub. "Look alive. We're going."

Everyone had set off, so I chased after them.

* * *

After walking for a little while, we came across an area marked EMPLOYEES ONLY.

Wood planks painted in all sorts of colors covered the area, and on the boards was written YOU CAN'T COME IN HERE.

It didn't matter if we were employees or not, however. We had the demon king with us. A spot in the wall of planks took the shape of a door, and we stepped right through it.

"It's just a construction site," I said.

"You are correct, Elder Sister. That is precisely what this is."

At first, all I could see was an old street, so I wasn't sure why the area was off-limits. But after we'd walked for about three minutes, the scenery changed drastically. The street ended, and we found ourselves at the edge of a vast wasteland.

A good number of demons were there, using pickaxes to dig into the ground.

"I see. So that's why it's off-limits."

We were now outside the theme park area.

"It would destroy the atmosphere if anyone saw what goes on behind the curtain."

"That is correct. It is considered inauspicious among the nightmares to have the machinations of their magic revealed," Fatla readily explained.

"The underground city of Yostos is still working to expand their borders. This is one of the sites where that construction is taking place~ They're building a new area inside the old city, which has been closed off for some time."

Pecora seemed well-informed. Maybe she'd come to inspect once before.

"And I think the place they dug up the tablet was, ah… Over there."

She pointed to a spot in the ground not too far away from us. And there, exactly where she had indicated, we saw someone pulling something that looked very much like a stone tablet from the earth.

What's more, another demon was bringing a pickax down on it!!

"Nooo! Stop! Wait! Hold on! Stop!"

I interrupted them in a panic and asked the demon in question to dig somewhere else.

"They're not preserving them? We almost watched a piece of history vanish before our very eyes..."

"Of course not. No one was ever able to read the tablets, so they're usually treated like rubbish~"

They must have been losing pieces of the past for some time...

"I think they should probably stop construction entirely, but...I'll leave that decision to you, Pecora..."

"Even if something outrageous were written on it, we couldn't exactly announce it to the rest of demonkind~ And it would be quite embarrassing if the contents proved to be unfavorable for the royal family~"

Aha. So there were political reasons, too.

Miyu and Smarsly went straight to the tablet and began deciphering it.

"Ohh, so that's how the grammar works. Gosh, that's so funny. These conjugations are way too difficult. Can you imagine trying to actually use these?"

Smarsly was hopping beside Miyu. Fatla had placed the keyboard cloth under it again.

"This must be written in verse. The number of syllables per line is the same. Does this mean they can only write in a fixed poetic form? That's sooo crazy inconvenient!"

Smarsly had been bouncing all over the cloth this entire time.

"Oh yeeeaaah. I wasn't really sure what that meant, but it seems to mean *incredible, mad, unbelievable, wild, surprising*, all in one word! That would be sooo crazy hard to use. Super crazy!"

That sounded a lot like how *some people* were using the word *crazy*. Miyu had absolutely no right to complain.

"Okay, I think I got it! Pretty easy, huh?"

"What's it say, Miyu?" I asked.

"It says, *Crazy. Just crazy. Totally super craaazy.*"

"If you didn't want to tell me, you could have just said so."

We Went to the Underground City of Nightmares

"Listen, translating ancient languages is, like, super hard."

I was pretty sure the problem was something much more fundamental. There simply *had* to be a more concrete way to phrase whatever she was saying.

Then Smarsly began hopping around on its cloth keyboard.

"What's that, Smarsly? *Carelessly trying to put the concept into words will cause the meaning to escape our grasp. The original word is so transcendent she is forced to describe it in vague terms.* Huh. Well, I guess I understand."

Maybe it was like how describing enlightenment with words only made it harder to understand...or something.

"Don't be fooled," said Beelzebub. "They are simply unable to interpret the language satisfactorily, so they are using overly broad language to cover for it."

Beelzebub was pulling no punches!

However, there were a number of other clay tablets, and Smarsly and Miyu were busy deciphering all of them. They probably couldn't spend too much time on each one individually.

"Incredible... Those markings do not even look like words to me, yet you can read them... This is not something I could do... I suppose there is good reason you are called a sage."

Laika was genuinely impressed. She was smart, insofar as she had really good grades in school (though that was quite impressive by itself), but she couldn't do something like deciphering a strange language. I couldn't, either. It was a superhuman feat.

"Right," I said. "There's nothing I can do to help here. I'll leave this to Miyu and Smarsly."

While the two sages were deciphering the tablets, Flatorte decided to take up a pickax and help with the construction. It seemed she had a lot more fun being active than she did sitting still.

As it turned out, the new clay tablets held a lot of information we hadn't known previously.

"*When the seal is broken, our god will be revived and save us from the deep dark.* That seems to be what it says," said Miyu.

That sounded terrifying...

"This one seems to be a prayer to the god. It even has what looks like the god's name."

"So we finally have a name... What is it?"

But Miyu shook her head. Smarsly hopped on its keyboard to spell out: "Unreadable."

"It's a special character just for the god's name, so I don't know how to pronounce it. Suuuper annoying."

These ancient beings were really making things hard for us.

"Oh! This one says where the god is sealed up."

Great! That sounds like a real breakthrough! If we can figure that out, we can shore up the seal so it doesn't come undone!

"Hmm. This is crazy. I have to solve a crazy-hard math problem to learn where the seal is. I swear, this just gets crazier and crazier!"

I got the feeling Miyu was going out of her way to work in the word *crazy* wherever she could.

The rest of us couldn't even tell it was a math problem, so there was no way we could help. I decided to leave the solution to the experts.

Miyu stuck a potato battery into her back.

"I totally need an energy boost! I swear, I *so* do not have the words to describe how crazy this is!"

Miyu put a piece of paper on the ground and sprawled out on her stomach, then began writing something very quickly.

Smarsly flew over the keyboard.

"Crazy, crazy, crazy, crazy, crazy, crazy, crazy, crazy, crazy, crazy!"

Wow! All she was saying was the word *crazy* over and over, but she was definitely writing out a very long math formula!

"Lady Azusa, I am so impressed...," said Laika. "I wish I could show Falfa... Seeing this has taught me once again that I have so much room for improvement... I want to take the next step forward..." She wiped away a tear.

"Is this really that inspirational, Laika...? I can tell they're doing something really difficult, but that's about it..."

Flatorte, meanwhile, had stopped digging and was sleeping on the ground. Apparently, this deciphering business was no big deal to blue dragons... No, that was being reductive. There had to be some blue dragons who were exceptionally smart, right? ...Right?

Thirty minutes had passed when Miyu placed down her pen and slowly stood.

"It's solved," she announced.

"So where is the seal?" Beelzebub asked.

"Well, if we assume the tablet was discovered in the same place it was originally buried, then it'd be over there, I guess. I can see some crazy-bright light, too. We probs need to guard that spot, or, like, something might come out."

Miyu pointed in the direction of some ongoing construction.

"Oh, no, that just happens to be a district they're working on," Pecora said breezily.

"Your Majesty, this is terrible! Will you not show even the slightest alarm?!"

"But panicking won't change anything, Beelzebub. A leader must remain calm and composed."

"There is a time and a place for everything!"

"I don't think this is the time and place for you two to be arguing! We have to hurry and go!"

We rushed over to the spot that supposedly housed the seal.

We have to get there! We have to make it in time!

Sure enough, the ground there was glowing with an unnatural brightness. I could tell right away that it was a special place.

"There! There it is!"

But as we got closer, we saw something ominous. The glowing spot was covered by a black cloth...

Pecora, undaunted, threw back the cloth. The earth beneath was a different color from the surrounding area, and we could see the traces of someone really going to town with a pickax…

"The seal is *definitely* broken!"

I held my head in my hands.

"Why would they start digging up land that was so obviously glowing? Didn't anyone think, *Hey, this is weird*, and stop?! And the ground around it has obviously been tampered with!"

The area around the spot was flat, as though it had been leveled. It appeared to be paved with something like marble. Not only that, it was literally emitting light. It was clear as day that this was a special place.

"A good majority of the demons who live here do not like the sun… I suppose they disliked this sort of light as well." Beelzebub limply fell to her knees.

Fatla held a hand to her mouth. This was quite the shocking situation.

For everyone except Pecora, anyway.

"Oh dear. It seems the seal is broken~"

She crouched down, casually peering at the spot where the seal was, like all of this was someone else's problem. She seemed utterly carefree.

No—maybe Pecora was simply trying to approach the situation calmly. She had to be aware of her position as demon king. She knew when to give up. And she was smart—she knew what was going on.

"There is a very high probability that this elder god has already escaped…but actually, I'm relieved."

She smiled. It didn't seem like she was joking around.

"What does that mean, Pecora…?" I asked.

"The seal seems to be broken, and yet nothing has happened to us demons or our territory. So either the elder god has no intention of doing anything, or it cannot act."

I suppose that's one way to look at it.

AN ELDER GOD WAS REVIVED

"That's true. At the very least, a calamity didn't befall the world the second the seal was broken or anything like that."

Even the underground city of Yostos—ground zero—was intact, not to mention the whole of the demon realm itself.

That probably meant the elder god hadn't exerted its influence yet.

"Now that we know the seal is undone, we can move to the next step." Pecora turned and smiled at all of us.

"Let's search for this elder god!"

Obviously, now that we knew the elder god had escaped, we couldn't just sit back and relax.

"The god may have escaped its seal, but it is probably unfamiliar with our time period. There is a very high possibility it is still wandering aimlessly nearby. Let's look around the city."

Pecora was right—we still had time. There were things we could do before the elder god started to act.

"But, Your Majesty," Beelzebub interjected. "We still do not know anything about this entity. How are we supposed to find—?"

Just then, Smarsly began to hop around.

"Oh, you have learned its unique characteristics from the clay tablets already? Very well. Tell us."

Smarsly hopped rapidly across its keyboard.

"The tablet said, *Our great god can infinitely change its form and appearance?*"

That sounded like something a god would do.

"Ugh… Infinitely change its form and appearance? We'll never find it…," I complained.

"Smarsly is not done. It still moves. *It is typically elliptical,* apparently."

Elliptical? That only made it sound stranger…

"And furthermore, *Our great god is infinite, thus in the image of infinity, it is unbound by form.*"

"This thing is gonna be impossible to find…"

But Smarsly wasn't finished.

"*Some gods believe it to merely be a poor artist, but that is baseless slander. It simply depicts eternity. The end.*"

That last part was very specific…

"So………I suppose this means there is a good chance this elder god is bad at art. Our hints will be in the pictures," Beelzebub said.

Though she was the one speaking, she also seemed a little perplexed by this turn of events. It was written all over her face.

"So how are we supposed to find it?" I said. "Do we ask everyone who lives in the city to draw for us?"

"Wh-what other choice do we have?! I am not the one who wrote those tablets! You'd best complain to their author if you are displeased with the idea!"

It was true that none of this was Beelzebub's doing, so I didn't press any further. Either way, we still didn't know how we were going to find this god.

"It is better than no hint at all," Pecora said. "I'll get us a little help. *Vosanosanonnjishidow vidiste fulco shizoni!*"

She began to mutter a spell. It sounded a lot like the one I used to summon Beelzebub.

Then a demon *poof*ed into existence in front of Pecora. I didn't know who he was, but he radiated an air of importance.

"Ah… How may I help you, Your Majesty…?" the demon asked.

"I have a little request for you. Do you think you could do this for me?"

The demon, unable to go against his king's wishes, said he would do what he could and ran off.

"Uh…Pecora? Who was that?" I asked.

"The mayor of Yostos."

"I see. I guess asking for the mayor's help would be the right thing to do."

"I told him to hold drawing contests throughout the city."

"That's not exactly what I'd call a request."

As the demon king, Pecora was rather forceful whether she meant to be or not.

"This will heighten our chances of finding someone terrible at art and should narrow down the scope of our search. Oh-ho!"

I felt this deserved some pushback. Since we were in a rather serious situation, I couldn't simply stand by and watch.

"Um, do you really think someone who's bad at art will enter a drawing contest? I'd be way too embarrassed, myself."

There were probably those who were unskilled but enthusiastic, and those who simply didn't realize they were bad, but most people who weren't good at something would be too embarrassed to participate.

"No need to worry, Elder Sister!"

But Pecora's confidence was unwavering. Maybe she had some secret tactic?

"We will cross that bridge when we come to it!" she concluded.

"I admire your optimism," I muttered.

"There is no point in worrying over whether or not they will draw for us! We must do everything we can right now!"

That was basically correct, so I had no more objections. There was no spell that could help us pinpoint bad artists, so all we could do now was wait.

Come to think of it, this might be enough information for someone divine to find who we were looking for.

When that thought crossed my mind, I wondered what my god friends were up to. I knew they tended to follow their whims, but considering there was a very real chance that an elder god had broken loose from its seal, I was a little nervous.

"I suppose we've done all we can~" Pecora stretched. "Let's retire to our hotel for today. I booked rooms for all of us at a nice place in the city."

"Well, we confirmed that the seal is broken, at least," I said. "I guess we did pretty well."

"I heard the breakfast buffet is really popular! I hope you're excited~!"

The world might be in danger, but for some reason I wasn't all that scared. I think I'd simply grown used to how things worked here.

Yeah. Everything would be fine. Hoping for an excellent breakfast buffet was the best thing I could do right now.

"And you're sharing a room with me, Elder Sister~! ♪"

Pecora said this very casually.

"Excuse me," Laika interjected before I could reply. "I am afraid that at times like this, either family shares a room, or each person should have their own."

"Well~ since there are two dragons with us, I thought it'd be nice for you to share a room. And so that's how I arranged it! ♪"

Laika was devastated. Meanwhile, it was Flatorte's turn to argue back.

"That's weird! I'm going to suffocate if I have to share a room with her! She's way too fussy!"

"How rude of you, Flatorte!"

"I can't help it if I find you suffocating! I know you're gonna nag me nonstop—'Don't make a mess,' 'Calm down,' 'Stop freezing things'—on and on!"

In my opinion, that was all common sense, no matter who she was rooming with.

I patted Laika on the shoulder.

"Will you make sure Flatorte doesn't get too wild and cause problems?"

"Oh, Lady Azusa… Of course. I know you need me to keep an eye on things, so…," Laika agreed somewhat reluctantly.

Pecora was chuckling the whole time. I had a feeling she'd orchestrated all of this.

It'd be nice if all this nonsense with the elder god was just one of her little ploys, too.

…Though I'd be pretty mad at her if she owned up to it after all this.

When we returned to central Yostos, we found all sorts of events encouraging people to draw things like mascots or scenery. It seemed the plan to smoke out this god via art was serious.

The tablet said the elder god could change their form and appearance infinitely. Would they even look like an intelligent life-form? What would we do if they took the form of a wall? We couldn't search for something that didn't even resemble a living creature.

Despite my worries, Pecora and I entered our room.

"Wow, how luxurious~ As expected of a developing city. ♪"

The first thing Pecora did was test how soft the bed was. She then went over to the second bed and pushed them together.

"Actually, I'd prefer we kept those where they were."

"Aww, but it's normal for sisters to sleep together~ It's good manners."

She kept calling me her elder sister, but she never listened to what I said... Then again, we were lucky we could argue over something as trivial as beds. And it was Pecora who was maintaining that carefree mood.

"Hey, Pecora, can I ask you something?"

Pecora was kicking her feet on the bed, like she was swimming.

"Yes, Elder Sister. What is it?"

"Don't you expect any danger in this situation?"

Pecora quietly took a seat at the edge of the bed.

"Why do you think that, Elder Sister?"

Did her reaction mean I was right? It was probably too early to tell. Maybe it was just wishful thinking on my part.

"Well, we're talking about a *god* who has been revived in your country, and we don't know what it's planning. It wouldn't be strange if you were a little more panicked. I know you might be putting on an act, but...you seem really calm."

Pecora was the demon king—she should be taking this situation way more seriously than I was. Even if she was trying not to worry the others, how was she so relaxed?

"You're mostly correct, yes. I do not believe this god is all that dangerous. My proof is that—"

She had proof?!

"—if this god were capable of plunging our world into danger, then even the gods whom the demons do not believe in would jump into action. You are on friendly terms with some of them, Elder Sister, and I am confident they would have told you something. But you only heard about the situation from us~"

She puffed out her chest proudly and continued:

"I only worship the demon gods, so I do not recognize the gods from other lands as divine. But I am well aware that they exist. This business with the seal is a problem for the whole world; if the elder god were truly dangerous, then the other gods would be taking measures of their own to stop it."

"That makes sense. I was thinking the same thing." I nodded slightly. "I was a little worried that I hadn't heard anything from them, but if you look at it another way, maybe they aren't responding because it isn't important."

This felt like the kind of situation Godly Godness or Nintan would have alerted me to, but I still hadn't heard from them. And besides, it was best to let gods deal with their own affairs. The demons and I shouldn't get involved.

"Phew. That's a weight off my shoulders," I said.

—But then a rift appeared in the middle of the room, and a moment later, Godly Godness and Nintan stepped out.

"This is terrible, Azusa~! The seal on an old god has come undone!"

"Azusa! An elder god has been revived! This is bad!"

They're going to tell me *now*?!

"O-o-o-o-o-o-oh no…"

Pecora collapsed back onto the bed. She must have realized how bad the situation was at last.

"Hey, come on! You've got to tell us these things earlier! Pecora wasn't taking this very seriously, and now she's fainted!"

"Sorry~ We tried to resolve this secretly among ourselves, so we were a little late in contacting you."

I felt sure organizations were not supposed to do that.

"Indeed. Things have gotten out of hand, and We could no longer keep quiet about it. Thus, We have come to inform you of the situation."

That was the last thing I wanted to hear right now…

"We've been aware of the elder god's revival for some time now, but since it can change its appearance at will, We haven't been able to locate it. We believe it is hiding in this underground city…"

"Nintan, can't you use your divine powers to find it? And what is this elder god anyway? Do you know its name?"

"Do not ask Us so many questions at once! It is difficult to answer!"

When Pecora woke up, she and I listened to what Nintan had to say.

"First, though it is referred to as an elder god, that does not mean it is any older than the other gods in this world. It simply happened to be here when the world was created."

"Yes. A colleague of Nintan's. You know, like a former employee who retired."

As always, Godly Godness's comparison was a little too casual for the situation.

"Many gods presently live in this world. There are those who work very hard, those barely scraping by, and those who sleep in seclusion. But this god's views did not line up with ours."

"Like a band breaking up due to creative differences."

Godly Godness kept interjecting, making it hard to concentrate.

"It is unique and has a hard time conforming. That in itself is not a bad thing, but allowing it to do as it pleased would have caused this world to develop in a bizarre and unpleasant direction. With no other choice, We sealed it deep underground. That is why it is called an elder god."

So even the gods called it an elder god. What a stunning coincidence.

"Yes, if only you'd resolved the conflict more peaceably at the time, you would not have to panic today~"

"Godness, become a frog."

Nintan had been pushed beyond her limit, and a cold white light shot out from her hand. When the light hit Godly Godness, she was once again turned into a frog.

"Oh, this is a rare variety of frog, ribbit! How lucky, ribbit!"

"Godly Godness, if you're just going to get in the way, then please go home…," I said.

It didn't matter that she'd helped me before; if she kept acting like this, I would have a hard time continuing to believe in her.

"For your information, the elder god was not forcibly shoved underground. We offered it dominion over a portion of the underground and told it to do as it pleased. The seal—or rather, the boundary—is like a wall, erected so that there is no confusion as to where their dominion ends."

"Meaning the wall was broken."

"Back in the day, we did not anticipate development reaching this far underground."

Godly Godness occasionally stuck out her frog tongue, distracting me.

"If I may, judging by what I've heard so far, it does not sound like this elder god is much of a threat, no? You are saying you sealed it away peacefully?" Pecora asked Nintan, clinging to hope.

"Yes, but that was a long time ago. We do not know what it is thinking today. And it controls all the intelligent life beneath the earth. It would be bad if such things came to the surface."

I got the feeling Nintan had just blurted out something rather astonishing.

"So, Nintan, are you saying there are people living in the ground below us…?"

This was the first I'd heard of such a thing. In a way, this news was just as shocking as that of the sealed god.

"I do not know if they can be called 'people.' Their form is very different from your own. This is simply conjecture, but—if a regular person were to see these beings, their mind may shatter."

That sounded terrifying!

"Gosh, that sounds an awful lot like the myths about Cthu-something-or-other, ribbit!"

Godly Godness had just said something only I could understand,

An Elder God Was Revived

but I agreed with her. There was something down here beyond our imagination…

"Ummm~ If I may ask a question?" Pecora timidly raised her hand. "There are other gods, yes? Are those gods also working to stop this one?"

Now that I thought about it, I didn't know any gods besides these two. Wouldn't an infinite number of gods be able to do something about this?

"She's right," I said. "From what you've told us, it sounds like even the gods from the same generation as this elder god are still around. It'd be really great if we could get their help."

Nintan looked away.

"………The others insist that it is not their responsibility and that gods should not exert too much influence on mortal affairs. It seems they have decided to stay out of it."

Sheesh, talk about selfish!

"And so we, the goddess and the frog, have been searching for this elder god, but we're still having trouble."

The way Godly Godness described the two of them made it seem like a frog was her default form.

I decided to think positively: Two gods on our side meant we had the advantage.

Come to think of it—there was still one thing I hadn't asked.

"What's the name of this elder god, Nintan?"

It sounded like there were many other gods in the world, so if it had a name, that's probably what we should call it.

And there was a small chance that someone was staying at an inn under that name. I doubted anyone would check into a hotel as "Elder God," at any rate.

"Its name? Dekyari'tosde."

"That sure is hard to say…"

Maybe I should just stick to 'elder god'…

The next day, we split up and scoured the underground city of Yostos for this Dekyari'tosde, the elder god.

That said, it could apparently change form at will, so we couldn't base our search on looks alone.

Not only that, but since we were in the demon lands, the people came in all shapes and sizes. If this were a human city, everyone would look more or less the same, and we could have easily chased down those who stood out, but…

"Hey, Beelzebub, aren't that guy's horns just a little too long?"

"'Tis a normal length."

"Isn't that minotaur's head a little too big?"

"'Tis simply his build. I do not have the courage to ask him if I may investigate his head merely because it is a little large… He may be self-conscious…"

"Don't you think that demon's tail is a little too long?"

"I have heard that letting one's tail drag on the ground like that is quite painful. It does seem rather long…"

…It was hard to tell by appearance alone, since the demons were so diverse.

"I suppose 'tis truly impossible to try and pick out particularly strange passers-by."

"Yeah. And if this elder god is still hiding somewhere in the city, I think I understand why they don't want to cause a ruckus."

Beelzebub looked at me questioningly, so I explained.

"I mean, you can look like anything here, and they'll accept you. This elder god was so unique that it broke off from the other gods. Maybe a place like this is more comfortable."

I doubted there were demons like this back when the elder god was sealed away. Maybe it felt like the world had grown closer to its ideal while it was gone.

"That would be nice… But hell's bells, this elder god is giving us quite the headache. If only it would let us know that it had no intentions of causing any trouble."

Considering Beelzebub was a demon minister, that seemed like a genuine sentiment...

"I suppose 'tis well enough that our morning search has yielded no results. We shall put our true strategy into motion this afternoon."

"True strategy?"

"We shall seek out terrible artists. We are holding events all across Yostos asking people to draw. It's reasonable to expect at least one drawing by afternoon!"

We already had the help of two gods, and yet our Plan A seemed to be full of holes...

That afternoon, we all gathered in a room at the Yostos city hall.

All the pictures collected from the contests around the city were being brought to us.

"Drawing Contest: The Streets of Yostos, Draw your Mommy!, Design the Underground City's Official Mascot, Twenty percent off if you submit an illustration! ...They really were just trying to get people to draw, huh?"

But I doubted an elder god would have a mommy, so that one seemed like a bust. And just as I'd predicted, all the drawings seemed to have come from children.

"The submissions for drawings of the city are all boring~ None of these exhibits any sort of talent. You have to do more than simply draw scenery."

Pecora was so harsh... I wondered if the demon king was skilled in the arts as well.

"Your Majesty, the mascot portion isn't much better. This one seems especially doubtful. It consists of a circle with sticklike hands and legs— that is all. I wish they would understand that less does not always mean more."

The demons were acting like real contest judges. Weren't we supposed to be doing something else? They weren't the only ones, though— there was someone else here getting carried away.

"*You have drawn well and carefully. I see originality in your color choices.* That is all the feedback I have. Next picture."

"Laika, you don't have to critique every single one! That's not what we're here to do!"

There were more important things for her to focus on.

"Oh gosh. This is very inappropriate. I can't show this to any of you, so I'm going to throw it away."

"People really need to think about propriety. No matter the era, there are always idiots who think art is all about shock value. Even some of the gods."

The gods, too, seemed a little distracted. I was starting to get nervous. They seemed to be taking each entry way too seriously.

"I guess trying to find someone bad at art wasn't such a good idea after all..."

Since these contests were open to anyone, it only made sense that most people who entered would be those who were skilled or who liked to draw. It seemed unlikely that someone bad at drawing would even enter. The idea was obviously flawed from the beginning.

Sighing to myself, I flipped through a stack of self-portraits. They were mostly pretty good, though I had a feeling many of the entrants had purposely drawn themselves better-looking.

Then, mid-flip, I froze.

The portrait in front of me was neither good nor bad—it was like someone had randomly drawn lines all over the place.

"Whoa, what is this? Abstract art? Postmodernism?"

When I went to the modern art section in museums back in my previous life, I remembered seeing a lot of pictures of circles or squares, or where the paint was just poured onto the canvas—things I had no idea how to appreciate. This was like those.

Such pieces often had abstract titles as well, like *Work 1* or *Work A*; maybe that was some kind of rule. In my opinion, they'd tried too hard to be unique and ended up all the same.

It seemed the demons had that kind of stuff, too.

"Hey, Pecora. Does this count as art?"

I showed the portrait to Pecora, since she seemed to know what she was doing.

"No, Elder Sister," she said immediately, waving her hand. "There is hesitation in the lines, and the image is meaningless. There is no imagination, no effort. I doubt it counts as a picture."

She was surprisingly strict... That last part even seemed unnecessarily cruel. Maybe in the past, someone had told her such a picture *was* art, and it had irritated her.

But the picture in question was in the self-portrait pile. What about it counted as a self-portrait? Did the person who drew it actually look like that? Or was it a representation of what they looked like on the inside?

"Oh! Lady Azusa, is that the same artist as this picture?" Laika held up another drawing that was also just a mess of lines.

"Whoa, that's awful... What was the theme for that one?"

"My Ideal Image of the Demon World's Future."

"Yikes!"

"Hey, Azusa!" Beelzebub called out. "Check the name of the artist on those two!"

I looked at the name box. "Uh, sorry, I can't read demon script."

"You are wrong. That is not demon script."

Wait, could it be...?

When Smarsly saw the writing, it began hopping like mad.

Miyu rushed over. "Omigosh, this is crazy! That's the same writing as the clay tablets!"

There was probably only one person who could write in that language.

"And this is the special character they used for the god. That's why I had nooo idea how to pronounce it."

"Give it to Us!" Nintan immediately checked the name box. "It says Dekyari'tosde in the ancient script. This is it!"

So that *was* the name of the elder god!

"Is there anything written in the address box?" Beelzebub asked. "We might be able to find out their location!"

Nintan flipped the page over.

"*Promised Hill Hotel, Room 505.* Is there a hotel here of such name?"

"That is a very fancy hotel in the Yostos Uplands," said Pecora. "The cheapest room goes for seventy thousand koinne per person, per night."

We'd finally found the elder god.

"I suppose it *is* worth trying every strategy...," Laika murmured, impressed.

"As long as it turns out all right in the end," I said.

We headed straight for the hotel.

The manager even gave us a description of the god.

He said, "Their face looked like a terrible drawing."

That seemed a bit rude considering they were a paying customer...

We asked for a little more detail, and he said their face and body were so chaotic that the sight made him uncomfortable. Apparently, it grew a little more warped with each passing day.

When we showed him the awful, weird drawing, he said, "That's the spitting image."

"Then that means they're actually pretty good at self-portraits~" Godly Godness sounded oddly satisfied.

"Right! Time to beat it up!"

"No, Flatorte, don't! It's too dangerous! At least come up with a plan first!"

In the end, we learned that it always had its breakfast delivered to its room, so we decided to come back then.

"If we approach it now and it escapes, it will be very difficult to search for it at night. We must approach it in the early morning, when its guard is most likely to be down."

Somehow, the plan sounded so petty when a god said it...

The next morning, after plenty of rest and recuperation, we headed for the room where the elder god was staying.

Not all of us were going in through the door, however. The two dragons, Beelzebub, and Pecora were on standby outside the hotel window. If the god tried to escape by jumping out the window, those on standby would chase them down. Only the two gods and I were making our way into the room.

The three of us slowly walked down the hall.

"Ooh... I'm nervous...," I muttered.

We were up against a terrifying god, after all. We had no idea what it would do.

"It's all right, Azusa," said Godly Godness. "You are much better at art than they are."

That doesn't really matter at the moment.

"Um, Godly Godness? Do you know what sort of person Dekya... this elder god is?"

The name was so unique that I'd already forgotten it.

"Well, I haven't been in this world from the beginning~ But since they're from Nintan's era, I suppose they're just as powerful as she is."

Nintan looked irritated, but what Godly Godness was saying made sense.

If the elder god was truly on the same level as Nintan, then Nintan and I had a chance of beating it. After all, I'd once bested Nintan myself.

"Dekyari'tosde is tricky to deal with. One never knows what sort of thing it might do. Do not let your guard down. And if it has been accumulating power deep down in the earth all this time, then it is entirely possible it has grown too strong for us to touch it."

That also made sense. Like Nintan said, we really shouldn't let our— Wait, hold on, *what was that, again?!*

"What do you *mean* it might be stronger? Shouldn't you have said that a little earlier?"

"I don't think that should come as any surprise... It is perfectly reasonable to think it may have been gaining power without our knowledge! It may have been sealed, but it was not frozen. It was simply forbidden from coming to the surface..."

"All right, that's enough. We're here."

It seemed we'd already arrived...

Godly Godness leisurely knocked on the door. "Good morning! We've brought your breakfast!"

We didn't have any breakfast, of course. I wondered if it was all right for a god to lie like that. Then again, since we were dealing with another god, it was probably fine.

What would come out and greet us? I was genuinely nervous.

I gulped.

Slowly, the door swung open.

On the other side of the door was—

—a slime.

"What...? That's...a slime, right?"

I was looking directly at it. The only difference between it and a regular slime was that it was silver.

"OH! Do I look LIKE a slime?"

A voice came from the creature.

"Um, is that you speaking...? It seems like your appearance has changed significantly from when you first checked in..."

I had no idea what was going on.

"OH YEAH! People kept being like, 'What the heck are you?' so I changed into something different!"

If the slime had changed its body, that meant it had to be Dekyari'tosde, right?! And what was up with the way it was talking...?

"DO YOU understand what I'M saying? This is our first meeting, so I'm not CONFIDENT in my language."

Was this...like how Muu's speech sounded a lot like an accent to me? Was this the same phenomenon?

"Oh-ho. You have long held no connection with this world, and it seems your speech has suffered~"

If that was how Godly Godness saw it, then she must be right.

"OH! You know I'M a god! Who are YOU?"

"I AM GODLY GODNESS. I AM A GOD."

Godly Godness was acting like she was trying to communicate with some foreign tourist.

"I LIKE FROGS VERY MUCH."

I guess she became fond of the little guys after being turned into one over and over. But was that something the elder god needed to know?

"WOW! AMAZING!"

And now the elder god was playing along?!

"Um, Your Divinity... Why are you a slime?"

I decided this would be faster if I asked myself.

"I can take on ALL sorts of forms," it responded. "I TRIED to imitate the people who live in this world. But everyone's REACTION was so strange! I thought it might be due to my lack of visual SENSE, so I TRIED out all sorts of things."

Now that the elder god mentioned it, I could see papers covered in weird drawings scattered all over the floor farther back in the room. Though I wouldn't have known they were supposed to be any more than lines if no one had told me otherwise.

"And these slime creatures have a very SIMPLE shape that seemed easy to COPY, so I TRIED it!"

That made sense!

"I see, I see~ This god can freely change its appearance, but with no visual sense, its attempts at taking a demon form resulted in some unidentifiable being. So it decided to settle for something simple—a slime. Now that I understand your circumstances, the mystery is not all that complicated."

Godly Godness roughly summarized the situation.

"EXCELLENT! ALL RIGHT!"

When I heard the silver slime's words, all my tension dissipated.

"But HOW did you know WHERE I was? HOW STRANGE."

Indeed, from the elder god's point of view, it must have seemed like a bunch of people found out where it was and suddenly barged in.

"It was because We realized your seal had come undone!"

Nintan came to stand before the elder god.

I had a feeling Nintan would move things along a lot faster than simply letting Godly Godness chat with it. It'd probably only take half as long.

"It's been a long time, Dekyari'tosde! Do you remember Us? You are the ruler of the underworld—We must keep you in line, otherwise— *Bwuh!*"

"OH NO!"

The elder god in slime form leaped right at Nintan's chest and tackled her!

Nintan fell flat on her back.

"Nintan! YOU're angry! I'M scared! If I run, I WIN!"

The silver slime turned on its heel (well, I wasn't exactly sure if slimes had heels) and leaped out the window.

"No! It's getting away!" shouted Nintan.

"Stop, Nintan," Godly Godness said. "It ran away because it thought you would harm it. You did not approach it properly."

"But if it brings strange creatures from the underworld up here, we will all be in terrible danger! We must act!"

"Based on our meeting just now, it seems good-hearted."

"Does a slime even have a heart?! One can have a good heart and still cause problems!"

This was an emergency, and now the gods were bickering.

I rushed to the window, where I could see Beelzebub and the rest of them standing in the hotel garden.

"Keep an eye on where that slime went!" I yelled.

"What?" Beelzebub called back. "Was that silver slime a new species? But, Azusa, slimes hardly matter right now."

Oh no. They didn't realize the slime was the elder god. Of course, no one had told them it had taken the form of a slime, so that was hardly their fault.

"That slime is the elder god! Chase after it, but keep a safe distance! Try not to stress it out too much!"

I wanted to believe the elder god didn't have any malicious intentions to destroy the world or anything. If it was considering something that terrible, it probably would have done it ages ago, and it wouldn't have introduced itself to us so casually, either.

"Can I fight it, Mistress?"

"Absolutely not, Flatorte!"

Anyone would think someone asking for a fight was a threat. And there was no telling if Flatorte would be okay going up against a god.

"We have no choice but to pursue!" Nintan grabbed my hand—and leaped out the window!

"Gaaaaaah! At least warn me first!"

"We are only jumping from a fifth-story window. You will be fine."

Still, I didn't like being dragged around.

"Elder Sister, the slime went over there! Toward that area being prepared for development!"

"Got it, Pecora! Thank you!"

Nintan, Godly Godness, and I rushed in the direction she'd indicated.

A shadow formed above us—Laika had taken her dragon form and was flying over the underground city.

Unlike the surface, the outdoors here didn't include an infinite sky. She might hit her head on the ceiling of the cavern.

"Lady Azusa, the slime is straight ahead!"

"Got it! We'll take it from here!"

We didn't know how much power this elder god had, so I didn't want Laika or any of the others getting close if there was even the tiniest chance a fight might break out.

That meant it was up to me and the gods—the ones really responsible for this mess—to settle the matter.

We pulled open a boarded door marked NO ENTRY to find a wasteland stretching out before us. There were no demons with pickaxes here, just an abandoned lot.

It was there that we found the silver slime.

"OH! YOU are here!"

"Elder god! Please, let's just sit down and talk! We can work this out!"

But once again, the slime flew through the air like an arrow, straight into Nintan's stomach.

"*Bwuh!* Why do you only attack Us? We do not understand!"

Nintan crumpled to the ground. If even Nintan was no match for it, we must be up against a powerful opponent…

"All I know is that YOU're angry, Nintan! I WIN if I can escape, so I need to get OUT of here!"

"Even if We were not angry to begin with, such abuse is more than enough reason… You hit…quite hard…"

"You *ARE* angry!"

The slime rushed away again.

"Wait, wait!" I called out. "Please don't run away!"

I chased after it as fast as I could.

"I have to dig a hole and ESCAPE underground! You won't find ME there!"

Wouldn't that just cause eldritch creatures to start spilling out into our world? I needed to stop it…

"And if I don't WIN, I'll be the LOSER!"

Next, the slime flew at Godly Godness. It might have been fleeing, but it seemed to think it still needed to attack its pursuers.

"Hah!"

Godly Godness deflected the attack, forcefully pulling her hands apart in a breaststroke-like movement.

"Whoa, nice one, Godly Godness!"

"Heh-heh, that's nothing for me," she said smugly. "But…that is all I can do."

In the end, she fell to her knees. "My hands hurt… My palms are stinging…"

"You're a god! Be more useful!"

"It's all right. There's still someone we can depend on." Godly Godness pointed at me.

"Uh, don't you know it's rude to point?"

"I'll leave the rest to you, Azusa."

………So this was it. It was all riding on me.

But it would be bad news for this world if the elder god got away. It seemed I had no choice.

"Um, elder slime god," I said. "We aren't going to hurt you. Please just hear us out."

"But Nintan IS angry. That's the face she makes when she says, 'We're not going to be angry with you, so just tell Us,' and gets angry ANYWAY!"

That was pretty easy to imagine…

"Forget about Nintan. Trust me! I'm very hard to anger. Instead, I tend to jump at any chance to compromise."

"I do not KNOW who YOU are!"

Of course it didn't.

"I'm Azusa, Witch of the Highlands. Er… Nice to meet you, I guess?"

My introduction made me sound a lot like a transfer student just arriving at a new school.

"I don't know what that means, but YOU are Nintan's FRIEND, YES? I don't want to talk to YOU!"

"I understand what you're saying, but please! Your actions could endanger the whole world!"

"If YOU do not get out of my WAY, I'M using force!"

The silver slime leaped at me!

This should have been obvious, since it was actually an elder god, but it moved much more quickly than a normal slime. It was so agile.

"Gaaaaaaah!"

I threw myself back, dodging the attack.

The slime hurtled some distance away, then came back.

I guessed it was trying to do some damage to me before running away. I wasn't sure if I should be glad it had returned instead of escaping.

"You dodged MY attack. YOU're quite quick FOR a god!"

"But I'm not a god. I'm just a witch trying to live a relaxing life."

Nothing about this situation warranted me bringing up my relaxing life, but asserting myself didn't cost me anything.

"Here I GO again!"

This slime was unbelievably fast. As it flew through the air, its round body morphed into the shape of a thorn. If there was such thing in this world as the ultimate slime, this would probably be it.

Still, I managed to dodge it again.

"Huh, I guess that worked…"

I could hear Godly Godness saying, "Wow! Look how cool you are, Azusa!" But I would have preferred she join the fight instead of just cheering me on from the sidelines.

"Your ultimate stats are the real deal! You're doing well! One god-tier dodge after another! It has to be god-tier when you're up against a god!"

"I'm not doing it consciously… My body's just moving on its own…"

Even if my stats were god-tier, I didn't think I had a skill or a spell that let me dodge without even trying. But in that case, what was going on?

"Oh, I know what this is!"

"…Do you plan to tell us, Godly Godness?"

Did she expect me to read her mind?

"You must have killed so many slimes that your very body has memorized their movements!"

* * *

"What? Is that a thing…? So you mean…"

"Yes, exactly! Your opponent has taken the form of a slime, thus limiting its movements! Thanks to that, your body can predict its attacks!"

To be perfectly honest, I wasn't sure I totally trusted what Godly Godness was saying, but I was, in fact, dodging the elder god's attacks.

"YOU ARE quite nimble! But I'M a god, too! I will hit YOU once!"

The elder slime god sounded fearless. Still, I kept dodging every one of its attacks.

It was so strange… It was as if I could predict the path of each strike, as if I knew where each hit would land.

At some point, Nintan got up.

"Bwa-ha-ha-ha! We see not even you can defeat Azusa, the Super-Divine Ultimate Weapon, the Violence Machine!"

"Don't give me weird nicknames!"

I wished she wouldn't make me sound like a monster. Violence Machine? No mother could raise her kids well with a name like that…

"Um, Nintan. Think you could help me out here?"

"We have never fought with anything so small as a slime before, which makes its movements hard to read. Therefore, We pass."

There were three of us, and yet I was being forced to fight one-on-one…

"Y-yes! That's right! Nintan and I cannot predict the slime's movements, and that is why we were defeated! There is no such thing as an overpowered slime, and so we were outwitted! It's simultaneously the strongest and weakest character—a god cannot handle such a paradox!"

"That may be a reasonable explanation, but I get the feeling it's still just nonsense…"

"You're perfectly suited for the job, Azusa! Everyone associates the Witch of the Highlands with slimes!"

"No they don't."

I had a feeling this was all just an excuse to make me deal with everything alone. But it was still true that I was dodging each and every one of the slime's attacks.

"Wow, HOW strange… I DON'T UNDERSTAND!"

After I'd dodged thirty times, the slime came to a stop.

"Please just let ME hit YOU! I'M speeding UP!"

Zoom! The slime flew right at me.

My body, however, reacted just as it had before.

I couldn't follow the slime's movement anymore, meaning my ability was positively supernatural.

I twisted, dodging each of its attacks and landing a light punch to what looked like its weak spot. Even this was mostly subconscious.

It connected, and the silver slime crashed to the ground. Smoke and dust rose from the earth.

"…I guess my body has adapted specifically to kill slimes."

I had three hundred years of experience, after all.

Now that I'd met a particularly powerful slime, I'd finally noticed my abilities. There just weren't any slimes that impressive. The only possible exception was Fighsly.

"Oh! **Slime Killer Azusa** did it!"

"I knew the **Slime Killer** could pull it off!"

"Please stop giving me weird nicknames! I don't want them to stick!"

That said, I could hear the happiness in my own voice.

It was true I'd had the advantage in this battle, and if I'd managed to force my opponent to step down, the situation would be resolved.

When the smoke cleared, the slime was still there. And since it was a slime, I had no idea if it was even injured or not.

"YOU ARE truly powerful! AMAZING!"

"Um… I'd be very happy if you acknowledged your defeat and listened to what we have to say—"

"But it sounds like the only reason YOU defeated ME was because you are especially strong against slimes! I can take ANY form I want, so I'LL just CHANGE!"

©Benio

Gah! That would mean I'd lose whatever bonus I had against slimes.
"Oh no! That's not good…"
"To think it would see through your weakness…"

"It's because you two goddesses wouldn't shut up!"

This was bad… I could only hope this didn't mean the tables would turn and leave us in a tight spot…

"I will CHANGE into a demon from this world!"

The elder god's body began to morph! It glowed, transforming from a slime into something tall…

…wobbly, and hard to describe. I couldn't understand what I was seeing.

It had winglike appendages, but they were stuck into the ground, and there were a lot of…tails? Sprouting all over it…?

One might very charitably call it a chimera, since it was incorporating elements from a whole mess of creatures. That said, I got the feeling that would be an insult to chimerakind.

"Heh-heh, I'M a demon NOW!"

I was pretty sure no demon looked like that.

"Dekyari'tosde, you haven't improved at all… You are terrible at this! You have no creativity!"

Now that Nintan mentioned it, the elder god's pictures were all made up of random lines, too…

"I WILL fight with this body! I WILL send YOU away and I WILL live a free life on my OWN!"

Was this gross, ugly-looking thing going to attack us now?

"I don't really want to fight you, but fine! Let's go!"

……

…………

For some reason, Dekyari'tosde wasn't moving.

"Hmm? Is it charging up an attack? That thing video-game bosses sometimes do?"

I steeled myself further. When it came to things like this, attacking first always led to being countered and beat to a pulp...

Come at me!

"I cannot MOVE!"

The elder god sounded pitiful.

Really? Was it telling the truth?

"I see. Your imaginative skills are so poor that you are unable to function as a creature. You are simply an object."

Nintan strode over to the god. Then she used what looked like a bright, glowing rope to bind the monster.

"I am tied up AND cannot move!"

"You could never move. Now you cannot transform into something else and run away."

We had successfully captured the elder god.

After confirming everything was safe, we called over Beelzebub, Pecora, Laika, Flatorte, Fatla, Miyu, and Smarsly. All of them believed the elder god to be a real monster and were shocked.

Its body *was* a mess.

"I feel like I'm going to have nightmares, Lady Azusa...," said Laika. "It must truly be a malevolent god..."

"That's understandable, since you've only seen it in this form."

"It looks sticky."

"I guess not even you want to spar with *this*, huh, Flatorte?"

We finally had time to talk, so the elder god told us all about its circumstances, and we, in turn, explained what we knew.

When the seal came undone and Dekyari'tosde emerged into the underground city of Yostos, it decided to play around a bit.

It didn't seem to have any desire for revenge against the world or Nintan and the other gods, though we'd kind of assumed as much once we found out it was staying at a hotel.

"By the way, do you have any demon money? That hotel is rather expensive~"

Pecora's question wasn't that critical, but it was something I'd been wondering, too.

"I learned that all I HAD to do was make shiny things, so that's WHAT I did!"

The ground at the elder god's feet suddenly turned into a lump of gold.

"I turned EARTH into gold. When I brought one in, they let ME stay as long as I LIKED!"

Its very existence was alchemy...

We asked the elder god not to connect the world of creatures it had created with this one. That was our greatest point of concern.

It readily agreed to our request. The elder god had no intentions of deliberately destroying the world, so the conversation went pretty smoothly.

Smarsly hopped over its cloth keyboard, spelling out a question.

"It wants to know specifically what sort of people live in the underworld," Miyu said, speaking on Smarsly's behalf.

"It's difficult to EXPLAIN. The underworld is full of COOL CREATURES I CREATED, enjoying life."

Suddenly, I understood everything.

A bunch of creatures that could damage one's mind simply by looking at them—they were all down there, deep inside the earth... They may bear us no ill will, but we must never seek them out.

I decided to never venture down below.

There were things in this world I had no business sticking my nose into.

* * *

"Now then, we need to decide how to deal with Dekyari'tosde, the elder god. What do you think, Nintan?" Godly Godness asked.

This was a divine matter, so it made sense that the gods would decide.

"Yes… The seal has been undone, so I think it would give Us more peace of mind if it was somewhere We could keep an eye on it…"

"Gosh, you can never just be honest with yourself, can you? Why don't you just admit you want to welcome it as a fellow god of the modern world?"

"Silence. Become a frog."

Whoops, Godly Godness was a frog again…

"Very well. Dekyari'tosde, you are coming with Us. Do you mind?"

"Not at ALL! I'm glad! There is so MUCH I want to learn about this place!"

I was worried for a second, but it looked like everything was going to be fine.

"Dekie, I'm glad things have worked out, ribbit."

"What did you say, frog?" asked Nintan. "What is *dekie*?"

"Dekyari'tosde is such a mouthful, so I'm calling it Dekie, ribbit!"

"That's not bad at ALL!"

With that, we decided to call the elder god Dekie. It felt a bit like calling a neighbor by a nickname. I wasn't sure that was appropriate for a god, but since so few people even knew its name, it was probably fine.

There was still one problem, though.

Nintan was looking at the elder god with an odd expression.

"We loathe the thought of leaving this place with you in that state; please take on a normal form…"

She had a point. If the elder god were to appear in the human world looking like that, everyone would think a malicious god had escaped. It'd cause a full-blown panic.

Just then, an idea struck me.

"We have a lot of options, don't we?"

* * *

About an hour later, Dekie picked out one of the pictures submitted to Yostos's original character design contest.

This, of course, was one of the contests we had held to smoke Dekie out.

"This one gets the elder god prize!"

Dekie stared hard at the picture as its gross, eldritch body glowed and morphed. At last, a divine being emerged that looked exactly like the picture.

She wore a large hat and a white robe befitting a god. Her hair was light green.

"Good! You look more like a god now."

"This body is much easier to move around in, YES!"

That new form looked like a lot of work, but I was glad she was happy with it.

"Omigosh, Dekie, I'm a sage, so like, I really want to know what it's like in the underworld. There must be sooo many clay tablets we haven't discovered yet!"

Oh, right, this was something Miyu was deeply interested in.

"OKAY, OKAY! In that case—*mfgh!*"

Nintan clapped her hand over Dekie's mouth.

"We shall share with you a more palatable version at a later date. If she were to tell you herself, your mind would shatter."

I bet the world was full of monsters that looked like Dekie's previous form...

Curiosity killed the cat, after all. It was better to be safe than sorry.

WE WENT TO AN **IMPROVED APPLE** EXHIBITION

When you receive an invitation from a demon, it doesn't mean *Come if you like*. It's a demand.

Just such an invite had arrived from Beelzebub.

This was an unusual notice. For once, it sounded like the kind of thing you would expect from a minister of agriculture. We didn't have any conflicts for the date given, so we decided to all go together.

Flatorte might get bored at a serious event, but these were demons

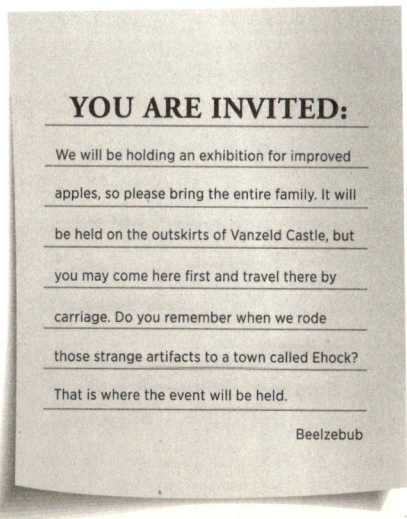

YOU ARE INVITED:

We will be holding an exhibition for improved apples, so please bring the entire family. It will be held on the outskirts of Vanzeld Castle, but you may come here first and travel there by carriage. Do you remember when we rode those strange artifacts to a town called Ehock? That is where the event will be held.

Beelzebub

we were talking about—this was bound to be another elaborate affair. At the very least, we would probably get to eat some apples.

With that in mind, we made our way to Vanzeld Castle, then headed to the event in a VIP carriage Beelzebub had procured for us.

"We're traveling so fast...," I said. "It took us three days and two nights to reach the town on those artifacts..."

Once again, our carriage was pulled not by a horse but by a behemoth.

"Indeed. Artifacts like those serve little practical purpose."

Beelzebub had been a victim of that incident, too, and she seemed to remember it well. I bet it wasn't cheap, either...

"Those artifacts are currently being tested out for use around the castle gardens," Beelzebub explained.

"Oh, so they *are* being used."

They looked like big creatures, so it would have been a little sad if they were left sleeping in storage. When it came to things like that, I couldn't help being influenced by appearances.

But Beelzebub brought a finger to her lips, indicating this was a secret. I guess that gesture meant the same thing no matter what world you were in.

"It cost quite a bit of taxpayer money, so we need to show that they are being used, or it would look very bad for us. We are doing everything we can to put them to use around the castle. 'Tis important that they appear to have some sort of meaning..."

"I'd rather not know what goes on behind the scenes with this stuff, actually..."

"Demons are all hale and hearty, which means they aren't useful for traveling short distances... I wonder if we could sell them to the human kingdom... Perhaps they might find use as a means of transport in smaller towns, such as for the elderly whose legs have grown weak. What do you think?"

"It's a nice thought, but I get the feeling it won't go over so smoothly... Either way, you should probably consult the government directly..."

I didn't really want to be standing at the front of a demon initiative that might throw human culture into disarray.

◇

While we chatted, we made it the rest of the way to the event venue at Ehock.

I thought it was going to be another festival, but from what I could see at the entrance, the atmosphere inside was more formal.

"The signage isn't very colorful... In fact, it's just the event name in black on a white sign."

The writing was in demon script, so I couldn't read it, but I bet it said, "Improved Apple Exhibition." There was a rough sketch of an apple in the corner of the sign, like an afterthought.

"'Tis an event attended only by those in the industry, so that is only natural. The usual guests include farmers, greengrocers, university researchers specializing in modified produce, and others related to the farming industry."

Beelzebub shot me a confused look, as though wondering how I hadn't realized this already.

"Wait. So then why did you ask me to bring the entire family?"

I had very little reason to come to such a specialized event, even by myself. I had no plans to plant any apple trees.

"The answer is obvious," Beelzebub declared, puffing out her chest.

It was? Had Sandra said she wanted an apple tree or something?

"To show the girls how hard I work! I knew you would not come if I told you to bring only the children, so I had you bring the entire family!"

"So this was all some lousy trick!"

I had a feeling Beelzebub had been growing increasingly sinister lately. She seemed more and more like a regular demon...

The girls, incidentally, had already received event guides from the demons at the reception counter.

"This is quite a big event. How fascinating."

"It seems plant research has come pretty far~! ♪ Maybe we can see some funny apples~"

"Apples are vivisected simply because they grow delicious fruit. How terrible. You have to be careful about such things, or you'll only suffer. Meanwhile, other plants add too much poison to their leaves to keep the insects away, only to be sought out for medicinal purposes. Balance is key."

Sandra seemed to see things a little differently than the other two. However, all of them appeared to be taking an interest in the event.

"...Well, all right. Now that the elder god has been taken care of, go ahead and show the kids how impressive you are as the agricultural minister."

"Aye. That's the idea!"

I guess I'll let Beelzebub take the reins today.

The ceiling of the exhibit hall was very high.

Inside, rows and rows of temporary booths had been constructed from wooden boards.

"This feels like an expo (from when I used to live in Japan)..."

These things were probably the same everywhere. The US, China—all the expos I'd seen on the news looked just like this, and I bet that was true no matter where you went on Earth.

"It's not just *like* an expo, it *is* an expo," explained Beelzebub. "Farmers and researchers have brought along all sorts of things related to apples. It may be large, but it's only a single hall. I doubt any of us will get lost, so you are free to roam as you please."

As Beelzebub spoke, there came a crunching noise from behind us.

Laika and Flatorte were testing out some of the sample apples.

"It is a bit sweeter than normal, which is nice. The aftertaste is very refreshing as well."

"Mm, tashty."

That was fast... The dragons always seemed in their element when it came to taste-testing...

"They have quite the appetites, don't they?" Beelzebub sounded astonished. "There are a number of booths providing samples, so they are free to eat as much as they like."

Falfa and Shalsha also reacted to the word *samples*.

"Miss Beelzebub, is there a place providing apple pie?"

"Shalsha wants some apple jam. Jam does not necessarily have to go on bread. It has all sorts of uses."

"Aye, yes, there is such a place. You are both VIPs, so there is no need to worry. I shall ensure you are brought freshly baked apple pie!"

That sounded like an abuse of power to me.

There was a proud grin on Beelzebub's face. I hoped she wouldn't spoil the children too much.

That said, the chance to try a variety of apple-based cuisine wasn't such a bad prospect. That was probably why Beelzebub had invited us.

"Last week, they held the cedar improvement exhibition. 'Twas not exciting at all…"

"That does sound boring."

"Someone was developing a cedar tree that gives off fifty times more pollen than normal."

"Were they making a weapon to kill humans with allergies?!"

The booth right in front of us had little sample cups lined up in rows, with an amber-colored liquid inside.

"Oh, apple juice samples! Don't mind if I do!"

We hadn't had anything to drink on the carriage ride over, and this was just the thing to quench my thirst. I gulped the whole sample down at once.

It was *super* sour.

"Whoa! It's burning my throat! It's like fire!"

"That is apple vinegar. You must drink it slowly, otherwise you will choke."

The possibility it might be vinegar hadn't even crossed my mind…

It was actually quite good if you didn't knock it back in one swallow, and it was well-received by the rest of the family.

"Oh, this is lovely! I feel a little more sober than before. Apple vinegar, huh? I bet this would sell."

Halkara's reaction was fitting of the president of Halkara Pharmaceuticals, and she handed what looked like a business card to the person at the booth.

"I didn't think she'd be doing business here… I guess anything can count as work when you lead a company…"

I bet creative careers like hers were less tiring and stressful than other jobs, and what I'd seen of Halkara's daily routine seemed to back that up.

"Halkara seems busy, so let's move on without her."

Beelzebub was showing a clear preference for the girls over Halkara, but the latter's business talks might take some time, so leaving her behind was probably for the best. And if we just stood there behind them, the person she was talking to was sure to start wondering what was going on.

That said, there was a chance that Halkara might cause trouble. In fact, she was much more likely to cause a huge problem than the girls.

"Hey, Rosalie? I hate to ask this of you, but could you check in on Halkara every once in a while and report back to me?"

"Sure! You go and have fun, Big Sis. I got nothing to eat, so I'll keep watch!"

Rosalie saluted me and flew off toward Halkara.

This was an apple exhibition, after all, so there were bound to be more samples ahead of us. Rosalie, then, would be our best bet for watching Halkara.

I kept watch over my daughters from behind. Beelzebub took the lead, followed by Falfa, who in turn was followed by Shalsha, with Sandra at the very back.

I had to give Beelzebub credit. She was really in her element. I certainly had no explanations or commentary to offer in this situation.

"Wow, it really is all apples, Miss Beelzebub~! ♪"

"Indeed, indeed~! ♪ The demon lands are generally quite cool, so they are perfectly suited for apples. I, too, have done all I can to widen the crop's possibilities."

I decided to let Beelzebub show off today. She should have her moment in the sun.

Shalsha, who had been walking behind Falfa, patted her sister on the shoulder.

"Sis, there's a very yellow apple over there. I have never seen a variety like that before."

Just as she said, there was a booth with apples in a shade of bright yellow, which was not a very apple color. There were slices laid out for sampling, so it couldn't have been because they were unripe.

"Ah yes, those apples were developed by a team researching new varieties at the ministry. They spent a long time on—"

Beelzebub was giving her spiel, but it seemed to me it would be faster to simply try them.

"Let's see!" I took a sample slice and tossed it into my mouth.

My reaction was immediate.

"This tastes like oranges!"

The texture was still apple-ish, but it tasted one hundred percent like an orange... My mind was in chaos...

"My explanation was cut short due to one impatient individual, I see. 'Tis an apple modified to taste like an orange. It is not easy to produce oranges here in the demon lands, so this gives the consumer an option for casual enjoyment."

"Is it really that easy to modify fruits...?"

"No. I believe the development team worked very hard on this. Though while it was produced in the ministry, 'tis the product of a very specialized team of researchers, so I had no direct involvement."

Falfa and Shalsha looked puzzled as they sampled the fruits.

"Oh! But Falfa does detect the faint aftertaste of apple behind the orange flavor!"

"This fruit appears outwardly to be an apple yet tastes like an orange—that means the flavor is not what makes an apple an apple. Shalsha doubts it matters much, but when I let it linger in my mouth like this, the orange flavor bleeds into my conception of an apple, and it starts to taste weird..."

What a perplexing fruit.

"Hmph. This apple is another victim of terrible experiments, isn't it?"

"Sandra, you're making this all sound really scary. Do you think you could tone it down a little?"

The apples at the neighboring booth were a bright, brilliant red.

"Wow! They're so pretty, like jewels!"

"How perceptive you are, Falfa~ Those were developed over many years in the remote farmland of the—"

I had a feeling Beelzebub's explanation was going to drag on forever again, so I went ahead and popped a sample into my mouth.

It was red, so I figured it was probably a regular apple.

But I immediately choked.

"That's hottttttttttt! Super spicy! My tongue has gone numb!"

"You are too impatient, Azusa! That variety was developed for demons who specifically like very spicy food!"

"I can't imagine a situation where you'd put apples in a super spicy dish. How are you supposed to use these?!"

"What may seem useless at first glance often leads to innovation. You must never say such things are pointless."

Now Beelzebub was lecturing me... She *was* the agricultural minister, after all...

These were the demon lands. They weren't modifying foods just so that they would taste better. I had to be careful...

"Hmph. It looks like an apple, but it is no longer an apple. It's the same as if you brainwashed a human."

"Sandra, what did I say about toning it down?"

When she started comparing the apples to humans, everything she said sounded terrifying.

I had a feeling we were going to be seeing a lot more weird apples—"brainwashed," as Sandra would say—that went beyond our wildest imaginations.

At least we wouldn't be bored.

As we moved forward, we started to hear a familiar lute melody coming from somewhere farther down the aisle.

It was Kuku, singing and playing at one of the booths.

"Are the apple blossoms blooming now where you are~? ♪ —Oh! It's Azusa and family! How have you been?"

I waved at Kuku and headed toward her booth.

"I had no idea you'd be here, too, Kuku. It seems this expo has everything, even mini concerts."

"Oh, no, I'm here at this booth because I helped cultivate some of these apples."

"What? Why would they need a minstrel...?"

Kuku held out a sample for me.

"Just try one."

I was a little scared after the last apple set my mouth on fire, so I gently bit into the slice.

"Hey, Kuku. Can I be honest with you?"

"Of course," she said with a smile and a nod, so I gave her my opinion.

"It's *awful!*"

I scrunched up my face as I gave my immediate impression.

"It doesn't taste like anything, actually. It's like I'm eating paper..."

I really wanted to know how she'd cultivated an apple with no taste.

"Yes, exactly. I grew these apples while playing sad music for them the entire time!"

It sounded a little like how people played classical music to encourage plant growth.

"You remember how Her Majesty started those magic broadcasts, no?" said Beelzebub.

"There are also artifacts for listening to music now, aren't there?" added Kuku.

That's right—this world now had video streaming, with items like CDs arriving a little later. It was Pondeli who developed the CDs.

"Thus, 'tis possible to keep music playing constantly, even if the musician is not personally present. Behold, the rewards of technological innovation," Beelzebub explained proudly.

"I can make the plants listen to sad songs on an endless loop!"

Kuku looked a little pleased with herself, too. I wasn't so sure this was something worth boasting about.

"But is there really any point in making bad apples?"

"What?" Beelzebub said. "We have discovered that music affects the resulting flavor. Isn't that incredible?"

"It *is* an interesting experiment, but…I wish you wouldn't ask me to eat bad food."

"Oh, Falfa, Shalsha?" said Beelzebub. "That variety is quite awful, so no need to try them. They're incredibly tart."

"You should've stopped me, too! You had more than enough time."

I knew it. I'm being treated like a guinea pig…

As I stood complaining, Kuku brought over another tray of samples.

"These apples were raised on the songs I wrote as a student when I was hoping to break out as a minstrel."

I was a little hesitant to try one, despite the offer…

Oh yes—I knew just the person for this task.

I called over Flatorte, who had been standing behind me, munching on apples, and had her taste them for me.

This had to do with music, so she would be the one most qualified to comment.

"Sure, I'll have one."

Flatorte bit into three slices at once. Dragons were wild even when it came to eating.

"Hmm… It's like…I feel the passion, but the flavor quality isn't quite there yet…"

"What a perfectly accurate description! That's exactly it!" Kuku exclaimed. "It has passion, but it's still an amateur! It tastes as though the apple is still only concerned with its own interests and doesn't yet have room to think about what its audience wants."

This conversation seemed a little out of place at a fruit expo.

"The passion itself isn't a bad thing," Flatorte continued. "It just needs a little more originality. I'm not really feeling that from this flavor."

"You're right. I get the feeling it hasn't been exposed to many different kinds of music yet."

Laika piped up with a question: "Um, those two are talking about apples, right?"

"I was wondering the same thing," I replied.

After that, Kuku fed all sorts of samples to Flatorte.

"This is an apple I cultivated with ballads by a very talented minstrel, written in the middle of their career after they started playing it safe."

"Mmm. It's solidly tasty but not very impactful. I don't think this apple would top any charts."

"I grew this one with songs by a popular minstrel group written just before they broke up due to creative differences."

"The flavor, texture, juices—they're not bad, but there's no unity."

"And I raised this one with songs by a minstrel who wasn't too skilled but knew how to ride the trends to a relative degree of success."

"I feel like I've tasted this somewhere before, but there's no personality to it. This apple will probably vanish in another two years."

* * *

This was a very strange way to discuss flavor.

It seemed to me that they were simply discussing the music Kuku had played and rephrasing it to be about the apples.

Laika and I sampled them all, too, but we couldn't make heads nor tails of any of them. At last, Laika put my vague feelings into words.

"Um, Miss Kuku? Do you not have any apples raised on iconic songs by incredible minstrels?"

"Oh, I'm afraid not."

"Why not?" I couldn't stop myself from butting in. "According to your logic, truly good music would make for extremely delicious apples! So why didn't you try doing that? If you had, you'd be feeding people tasty apples, and they wouldn't complain!"

But Beelzebub, who was standing next to Kuku, gave an irritating little scoff.

"You are constrained by stereotypes," she said. "You must take a step back from the belief that it is necessary for apples to taste good."

"I must disagree! Apples are supposed to be food, and as such, I believe every effort should be made to ensure they are delicious."

"Exactly! What Laika said! Why are you acting like we're shallow for wanting our food to taste good?"

I would have expected the minister of agriculture, of all people, to try to grow delicious apples.

Flatorte, however, looked as though she'd just awoken to some great truth.

"Mistress," she said, "if you cultivate apples with the preconception that they must taste a certain way, then you can make a decently tasty one, yes. But in the long run, that thinking will only lead to the decline of apples as a whole. Animals will get bored of them."

"Uh, I'm pretty sure apples aren't just some passing fad."

I got the feeling she was talking about music again, but she wasn't, was she? This was about apples, right? Or had we started talking about music when I wasn't paying attention?

Flatorte turned to look at Kuku.

"Listen to me. It's important to consider what your customers and the farming cooperative have to say, but you're the only one you can count on in the end. Your customers may suddenly get bored and leave one day, or they may change their minds and decide they prefer sour apples to sweet. You're the producer, and you've gotta trust in yourself. You've gotta follow your gut and make the apples you want to make."

"I understand. A farmer who has concentrated on making nothing but sweet apples cannot suddenly shift to making sour apples."

Okay, yeah, this was about music.

"Next time, I'll raise apples on recordings of minstrels singing their hit debut songs again after leaving the scene for twenty years and staging a comeback!"

"Yes, Kuku! That's good!"

I wasn't sure when it had happened, but it looked like the two of them were now master and apprentice.

Laika glanced at me.

"It feels strange to compare us to them, but I am thankful your teachings are so easy to understand, Lady Azusa…"

"Oh, well… I suppose I don't usually say anything too weird…"

We'd left the subject of apples far behind, but it seemed like the weird samples were still coming.

"Look, Shalsha, there are apple trees growing over there~!"

The girls had grown bored standing around Kuku's booth. Falfa grabbed Shalsha's hand and took off down the aisle.

Just as she said, there were apple trees sprouting up in one corner of the venue. I bet those things were costing them a lot of money.

I left after Falfa and Shalsha, and Beelzebub followed.

It looked like Flatorte and Laika would be hanging around Kuku's booth for a little longer.

I suspected that while Laika was a bit exasperated with the other two, she still thought she might learn something from them.

As I approached the apple trees, I spotted cat ears.

"Oh! Miss Azusa and family! It's good to see you!"

This booth was being watched by the undead catgirl, Pondeli.

"I had no idea you'd be here, too, Pondeli. Are you making apples for a crossover event with your games?"

Pondeli was now a famous game designer. "Yes!" she said. "I'd like all of you to eat these."

She produced an apple cut into eight slices—a common way to divide the fruit.

I couldn't exactly refuse to try it, so I took a slice and quickly threw it into my mouth.

Falfa, Shalsha, and Beelzebub did the same.

"This is just a normal apple," I commented. "It's nice and sweet."

Falfa and Shalsha were nodding as they ate. At last, we'd found a good, solid apple.

But then Beelzebub brought a hand to her mouth, her eyes brimming with tears.

"Mmmgh... My nose feels all prickly..."

What was happening now...?

"You got the special slice! A characteristic of this apple is that one slice out of eight will have a wasabi flavor."

"Just what do you have to do to cultivate an apple like that?"

"I bet this one would be a big hit at parties! No doubt about it!"

I was pretty sure they'd *only* be a hit at parties... No one just looking to eat an apple would want one like this.

"The flavor is quite strong, so I am going to go cleanse my palate...," said Beelzebub. "The booth at the tree beside us has normal apples—perfect..."

Now that she mentioned it, Pondeli's booth wasn't the only one with a tree—there were others. Did that mean the other trees were for different kinds of apples?

There were a lot of crawlers gathered at the neighboring booth. These were a kind of demon, too—they took the form of big green caterpillars and were quietly munching on the tree's leaves.

"I guess they're growing trees with tasty leaves here."

This was a line of thought very suited to demons, since they were so diverse. It seemed some demons came for the leaves rather than the apples.

"Precisely. Since these are for children, we paid careful attention to the taste and nutritional value."

At the booth was a demon with butterfly wings—Nosonia. If I remembered correctly, she was in the fashion industry.

"All sorts of people come to this thing, huh...? Apples have a broader appeal than I thought..."

"I simply wanted others to know leaves could be even more delicious, and so I came to exhibit."

I figured this was something only those with a larval stage could understand, but it sounded worthwhile. Still...leaves as a palate cleanser? I would have preferred the fruit, myself...

It seemed Beelzebub felt the same way.

"Nosonia. I'd like an apple for each of us. The fruit, that is."

"Okaaay, coming right up."

Nosonia took out a knife and cut off the top of each apple.

The inside was filled with nectar—no, scratch that. This was a watery liquid.

"These are for the adult crawlers. The inside of the fruit has been made into juice."

"I would not have expected that to work. Some of these improvements are simply unbelievable."

* * *

Nosonia stuck a straw, made of what looked like a plant stem, into the liquid.

"Here, now you can have apple juice any time you like. This product is supremely convenient—no need to go through the trouble of pressing the apples to make juice."

It certainly seemed convenient, but I was starting to wonder if it was okay to change a plant so drastically. Wasn't a god going to come down and smite them or something? But the demons didn't believe in gods like Nintan, so I guess it didn't matter.

I saw a cynical smile cross Sandra's face.

"Heh. I have never seen an apple so tainted with darkness. It is no longer fit to be called a plant."

Maybe this apple had lost something important…

The juice, by the way, was one hundred percent fruit juice, and it was delicious. Falfa and Shalsha were also impressed by its quality.

"Oh! Even better than freshly squeezed—the fruit itself has become juice. 'Tis simply delicious."

The palate cleansing was a success.

After that, we rested at the table in Nosonia's expo space for a little bit.

"This juice is so good~ This is it! This is exactly what I'd been looking for~"

"I suspect her juice is the reason that she has been placed so far back in the hall. People will reach her just as they grow thirsty."

Huh, so they actually thought about stuff like that.

It was around then that my attention drifted toward the neighboring booth.

I felt a presence—specifically, a lot of movement. When I looked, I saw the apple tree branches shaking rapidly.

"Uh... What's happening over there?"

I was curious, so I headed over to check it out.

When I arrived, I found Fighsly facing off against the apple tree.

"Yah! Hah! Hiyah!"

As one of the apple tree's branches flew toward her, she dodged by tilting her head to the side.

When I took a closer look, I saw that the tree's fruit was a dark black and appeared to be made of iron.

"Honored guests! All you need is one of these in your yard, and you can train all by yourself to your heart's content!"

"Yet another bizarre 'improvement,' I see."

"This tree was grown with a strong stubborn streak. It won't give up its apples no matter what! It will attack anyone who approaches with its weapon-like fruit!"

"That is definitely not what I want out of an apple tree."

Fighsly heard my comment and turned to look at me.

"Oh, Azusa. What do you think? If any of the training gyms in the human lands want a tree like this, I will send one over."

"I don't know anyone in training gyms, so I couldn't say what they want. And don't you need to pay atten—?"

I stopped mid-sentence. One of the heavy-looking apples had hit Fighsly square in the face!

"*Bwuh!*"

She'd taken one heck of a hit, and she promptly fell to the ground.

"Wh-what a good punch... I think I have a concussion..."

"See? I told you!"

Several slimes hopped over to Fighsly. These had to be her pets, Free Tuition (yes, that was what she called them).

"Azusa, the apples at the neighboring booth are not for eating— Oh, 'tis Fighsly. Look how out of it she is," Beelzebub said matter-of-factly.

She did not seem particularly surprised that the apple tree was on the attack.

"I think this is the first time in a long while that I've genuinely thought about how scary you demons are. If these are bad jokes, I'm not laughing."

Beelzebub stared hard at me. "I do not quite understand what you mean, but I get the feeling you're being rude."

Afterward, Beelzebub continued to show us around, and we visited all sorts of booths. As always, she was *very* nice to the girls.

Laika and Flatorte drank a great deal of juice at Nosonia's, and Rosalie came over to tell me that Halkara was about to reach the most exciting part of her business talks regarding the apple vinegar. It seemed such discussions really *did* take a lot of time.

And as for me—well, I made a surprising discovery completely unrelated to apples.

All kinds of demons came over to Beelzebub to say hello—

"Minister, it is nice to see you visiting." "Minister, we have harvested incredible sleeping apples thanks to you." "Minister, thank you for all your hard work at last month's meeting."

—and she handled each greeting with ease.

"Seems like you're doing a good job as minister."

"Why do you look as though you've reevaluated your opinion of me? I am the minister—why would I not be doing my work…?"

I tended to see her most often when she wasn't acting very much like a minister… She usually came to the house in the highlands on her days off, of course, so it made sense that she wasn't acting like an official.

"You're so impressive, Miss Beelzebub~!"

"You have opened Shalsha's eyes."

"You're not half bad."

The girls joined me, their eyes shining with respect. Beelzebub shot us back a lazy grin, which was considerably less dignified than before.

"See? See? I always do my best for you girls~"

"As the demon minister of agriculture, it might be better if you said you were working for the sake of demonkind instead… It'd be a real faux pas if you said you were doing it all for them in a public address…"

Of course, it was probably because Beelzebub spent most of her time chipping away at more boring work that they could hold events like this one.

I didn't know Beelzebub's full story as a bureaucrat, but she'd probably risen steadily through the ranks.

Then there came a flurry of footsteps.

"Boss, Boss! Phew, I'm so glad I found you!"

Vania jogged over to us. Her main job was as Beelzebub's secretary, so she probably had something to tell her in that capacity.

"What? The event should be running smoothly even without my constant management. Or do I have an emergency meeting—do you want me to return to the ministry immediately?"

Vania waved her hand.

"No, it's nothing like that. Though depending on how you look at it, it might be even worse. Oh, Miss Azusa's here! It's nice to see you. Are you tired of apples yet?"

"Oh, hi. Don't mind me. Go ahead and tell Beelzebub what the trouble is."

Her greeting was rather chipper, so I had a feeling the situation wasn't too dire.

"What happened, Vania? Spit it out."

Beelzebub didn't seem very tense, either. I could see she was confident that she had squared away all her work before coming here.

"Well, um… Two particular people have found their way into the event."

"Stop being so dramatic. Who are they? I don't know what you're talking about."

If it was two people, it probably wasn't Pecora.

"You know, *those* two. You know who I mean—your natural enemies."

"Yes, but *who*? I got rid of my political rivals years ago, and I doubt any of them would join forces to ambush me."

Vania dropped her voice slightly and said:

"**…Your parents are here.**"

* * *

Beelzebub's face instantly went pale.

I had definitely heard the word *parents*. I had high stats in everything, so I could hear the quietest whisper loud and clear.

"Secure them immediately and lock them in the meeting room. I can think of no greater nuisance than running into them while making my rounds..."

"But they aren't exhibiting—I have no idea where in the hall they might be... Though I have received word from a ministry staffer who saw someone wearing an awfully wide-brimmed hat, so I believe they are indeed here..."

"No one else would wear clothes so obviously from the countryside... Unfortunately, you may be right..."

This had me genuinely curious. I dropped my own volume a bit so the girls wouldn't hear me.

"What? Your parents are here, Beelzebub? I want to meet them! You have been a help to me and the family, in one way or another, so I want to thank them. And you've bought my daughters so many gifts."

"For once, I would rather you act a little less like an adult! I shan't let you see them!"

"Do they speak all properly like you do? I'm so curious about them. Are they, you know, like, nobility?"

"Inquire no further! I have nothing to say to you! Do not stick your nose in another family's business! Furthermore, I believe I told you that I come from a common background! It was when you visited my manor."

"Oh yeah, now that you mention it..."

I'd been so fooled by her pompous way of speaking that I'd totally forgotten...

At any rate, the way she kept turning me down made it clear she was serious—she really didn't want me to see them.

She scratched idly at her cheek—she seemed to be thinking hard about what to do. Then, as though she had no other choice, she grabbed Vania's arm and turned to look at my daughters.

"I apologize, girls, but I have business I must attend to. Vania will be your guide from here on... If you need *anything*, just let her know, and she will do it for you."

Beelzebub was voluntarily cutting down on her time with the girls. This had to be a pretty big deal...

"If I hear that Vania was unable to guide you to your liking, then I shall deal with her when we return to work."

"Boss! Don't you think that's an abuse of power?"

I wanted to think Beelzebub was joking, but I had a feeling she was dead serious...

The girls all responded, believing some issue had come up with Beelzebub's job.

"I see. Work must be busy. Perhaps the apples have staged a revolt."

"Thank you, Miss Beelzebub~!"

"This has been very informative. I would like to thank you for serving as our guide."

Vania had been very quiet when she was speaking about Beelzebub's parents, so the girls had no idea what was really going on.

I wasn't sure what to do, but it seemed like this might be my only chance to meet Beelzebub's parents, so I decided to follow her.

Her reaction was immediate. She whirled around to face me and said, "You cannot come! Absolutely not!"

"Wow, this is a bigger deal than I thought... If things are really that complicated with your family, I'll stay put. I wanted to at least say hi, but..."

"Wait. I am not hiding a dark past. My childhood was normal, and we do not fight. I simply do not want you to see them... And I do not like you getting suspicious for no reason..."

"Oh, okay... Well, some parent-child relationships seem normal and problem-free from the outside but are very complicated for those involved."

Apparently, that was something humans, demons, elves, and dwarves all had in common.

"Indeed," she said. "You take care of the girls, and I shall—"

Just then, we spotted a very large straw hat moving toward us.

It was *huge*, which made it stand out. There was no way I could miss it.

"Hey, Beelzebub? Does that hat belong to one of your parents?"

Beelzebub whirled around—

—and immediately spun back toward me.

She was even paler than before.

Older games would sometimes distinguish the difficulty of enemy characters by giving them different color palettes at the beginning, middle, and end of the game—Beelzebub's face had gone so white that she looked like a higher-level version of herself.

"Oh! Beelzebub! How're ya doin'?!"

Two demons were approaching us—a man and a woman, both vaguely resembling Beelzebub. They appeared to be a married couple.

What's more, they looked like they had come straight from the countryside. Though I suppose it wouldn't be all that far-fetched for a couple of apple farmers to be visiting the expo.

Beelzebub was staring blankly into the distance.

I had never seen her make such an expression.

"Y-you have the wrong person... I am not Beelzebub...," she said, trying to brush them off and make her escape.

"I think I know mah own daughter's face. We been talkin' 'bout puttin' some of them weird apples in the store. I know, Beelzebub! Show us some good'uns!"

The male demon had started speaking to her, and I was certain he'd used the word *daughter*.

"Beelzebub, whena-hanna, haddem abbouta to!"

Now the woman was speaking...but I wasn't sure what she was saying. Was that some kind of regional dialect...?

Beelzebub buried her face in her hands as the man turned to look at me.

"Ohh, you our daughter's little friend? You don' look demon. Are ya some kinda bigshot from the human lands?"

The woman turned to look at me, too.

"Beelzebub'm deffa, tellum yar!"

"I'm sorry, I don't understand what you're saying... I'm Azusa, Witch of the Highlands... Beelzebub's friend."

I wasn't entirely sure how I was supposed to introduce myself, so I tried to play it safe.

"Gaaaaaaaah!"

Beelzebub screamed. I didn't think that was a noise the minister of agriculture should be making.

"It's all over!!"

She then grabbed the man's and my hands—

—and rushed through the expo hall toward an empty meeting room. I had no choice but to follow.

"So yer the girl called Azusa! Heard lots and lots about ya!" said the man.

"Watter feefler! Sheez mers!"

The woman spoke, too, but I couldn't catch anything she said...

"Oh yes. I am the Witch of the Highlands. Are you Beelzebub's parents? Your daughter always takes very good care of me and my family. You are both quite different from her."

The man burst out laughing.

"Well, yer right there! We're yer run-o'-the-mill farmers! Our daughter's yet to be paid for all'er actin'!"

"Yee, ahr! Dresnel!"

I didn't know what the woman was saying, but I could tell she was laughing, too.

"I—I see... But, Beelzebub, I don't understand what your mother is saying to me..."

"Azusa, Ma just said their house is a plain old farmhouse. 'Tis normal you do not understand her. I doubt anyone in the town around Vanzeld Castle can."

Things were happening so fast that I had no idea where to begin! But there was one thing I simply had to ask first—

"Um, Beelzebub. Did you just call your mom 'Ma'?"

"If you say any more, Azusa, I will curse you for a thousand lifetimes."

Apparently, that topic was off-limits...

Beelzebub told me everything in the empty meeting room.

"I believe I've told you before that I have not always acted in this manner, but I still loathe the idea of you meeting the two of them."

Beelzebub glanced over at her parents.

"I am not embarrassed by the countryside—I am embarrassed by *them*!"

"What's so embarrassin' 'bout us, mmm? Our business's doin' good!"

"Inne black an' fennin' drew! Drewin' fenn!"

Beelzebub's face went red again.

"No! I speak not of your business! I am embarrassed at the prospect of showing you to others! But you have no idea!"

After she buried her face in her hands again, Beelzebub pulled out a piece of paper and slid it toward me.

"Write an oath. Swear that you will not speak a word of this to any other soul."

I knew that if I broke this promise, it would ruin our friendship forever.

"...Okay. I won't tell anyone. I swear."

The problems between parents and children sure were complicated.

The day's expo went off without a hitch (probably).

It would apparently continue over the following two days, but the rest of the family and I would be returning to Vanzeld Castle that day and then going home the day after.

Beelzebub and I returned to the girls.

"Miss Beelzebub! The apple pie was really tasty!"

"This was truly a great day. Shalsha would like to express her deepest thanks."

"Aye, yes! 'Tis your smiles that give me life!"

Beelzebub might act all chipper in front of the girls, but I knew she had secrets she didn't want anyone to know about. This was a very serious matter for her, and I swore to never bring it up, no matter what. Vania seemed likely to let something slip, but for now, everything was fine.

"Oh yes. That's right. Miss Azusa?"

When Vania called my name, I jumped. She wasn't going to talk about Beelzebub's parents, was she…?

"There is a small group of individuals gathered who have business with you. I would like to take you to them."

"Huh…? What do they want?"

The first person I thought of who might want something from me was Pecora, but Vania had mentioned a group. Who could it be?

"It's not demons wanting to test their might against me, right?"

"No. They are not even demons."

Still unsure of what she meant, I was taken to an empty lot behind the expo hall. Once there, I finally understood.

Waiting in the empty lot was a little group of basilisks and deer.

"It's all the friends we met while riding on the robot kaiju!"

I had no idea they'd come all this way to see me. I went and patted all the deer on the heads one by one, and I did the same for the basilisks. I'd thought they were unusually comfortable around me, and it seemed like I wasn't wrong.

The rest of the family pet the deer and basilisks as well. Some seemed happy; others looked a bit frightened. Sandra, in particular, probably had to worry about deer nibbles…

"Wow! The deer and the basilisks eat apples, too~!"

Falfa's eyes shone as she watched a basilisk munch on her offering. It was like a little petting zoo.

Vania brought over some more fruit, and we gave those to the animals, too. This was an apple expo, so they probably had a lot of leftovers.

"Yes, eat up! Eat up! These are the tastiest apples in all the land! Any animal or monster would rush straight for them! Yes, these are Demon Apples!"

Beelzebub seemed pleased by the animals' reactions. She was the minister of agriculture, after all. She might have her secrets, but there was no doubt she was great at her job.

There was, however, one thing I really wanted to say to her right now.

I tapped Beelzebub on the shoulder.

"Mmm? Yes, Azusa?"

"If you knew about an apple that delicious, why didn't you show us that one first?!"

She'd taken us to all the weird apples instead! I'd never even heard of this one!

"Oh, right… There were so many varieties, I simply forgot."

"Give one here, now! I want to eat it!"

The apples I ate with the deer and basilisks were the best I had all day.

"This. *This* is what I've been searching for."

"'Twould not be much of an expo if we only had the one kind."

As the event came to an end, I was reminded that there was a reason some roads were more well-traveled than others.

WE WENT TO A CAT CAFÉ

A wyvern touched down near the house in the highlands. Just as I was wondering who it was, Nahna Nahna from the Thursa Thursa Kingdom appeared. She was alone.

"Hello! Oh? Is Miss Muu not with you today?"

Laika, who had been training outside, was the one to greet her. I was taking down the laundry.

"No, she isn't," Nahna Nahna replied. "I come bearing only an invitation, and I alone am enough for that. Her Majesty, who is planning the event, is presently incapable of thinking of anything else, so she has opted not to come today."

"Can't think of anything else…besides what? It isn't gambling, is it…?" A worried look crossed Laika's face.

Indeed, it wasn't very long ago that we witnessed someone face terrible losses in gambling… And Laika was the type to disapprove of delinquent activities.

"Oh, no. It's something else entirely. But I cannot tell you what."

"You cannot? Why is that?"

Laika tilted her head. Anyone would be curious.

"In Her Majesty's words, 'More fun that way, innit.'"

Well, I couldn't argue with that reasoning. Laika seemed satisfied as well.

"Thus, it is Her Majesty's fault. If any of this displeases you, then feel free to hold her in a headlock next time you see her."

Though spiteful as always, Nahna Nahna was still doing her duty by Muu, even if that meant she was at the mercy of her sovereign's every whim. She must be a very kind person.

"My strength is not for tormenting the weak...," said Laika. "But let us speak somewhere more comfortable—why don't you come inside? Lady Azusa! You have a vis—"

"I know, I know. I heard everything."

I had finished taking down the laundry, and so I made my way toward the others.

"If Muu's preventing you from saying anything, Nahna Nahna, then I won't force it out of you," I said.

"In my opinion, it is not exactly a secret worth keeping, so I think it would be perfectly fine for me to tell you."

"Whoa! There's no need to spill the beans. Muu might be more disappointed than you think. Plus, I don't want to feel guilty for hearing."

"I'll give you a hint—"

"I know you're just going to tell us the answer. You really, really don't have to say it!"

This woman had quite the stubborn streak, and she was not easy to manage.

"To avoid revealing the secret, I will simply tell you that Her Majesty has begun a little project. Something akin to a shop. You must drop by if it strikes your fancy."

That sounded plausible and casual enough not to warrant the sovereign herself making the trip here.

"I just have one question," I said. "Whatever it is, it's not dangerous, right? Can the whole family come along?"

Events held by demons, ghosts, and gods often involved elements that could harm normal people. That was the one thing I wanted to double-check.

"Oh, no. You should be all right."

Nahna Nahna's answer was immediate. In that case, our conversation was pretty much over. We were done before she even came inside.

"They are all very tame."

"...Tame?"
That wasn't a word I was expecting.
Still, I had a feeling if I asked any more, the secret would be spoiled, so I held my tongue.

◇

The following day, I and the rest of the family made our way to the Thursa Thursa Kingdom.
I was riding on dragon Laika's back. Falfa and Shalsha sat behind me.
"Shalsha, Shalsha, what do you think we'll be doing?"
"It's a secret, which leads Shalsha to believe it must be some great discovery. Perhaps magic that can easily bring the dead back to life or a spell that can rewind time."
"Wooow! She's going to revolutionize both science and arcanology!"
The girls' expectations were ballooning out of control.
"I don't think you should get your hopes up, kids... She might just be feeding us a nice meal... And bringing people back from the dead would shake the world's very foundations, which frankly sounds a bit terrifying..."
If such technology existed, Nintan or one of the other gods would probably have something to say about it. An innovation like that could turn the whole world upside down.
I was surprised to see another family member frightened by what the girls were talking about.
It was Rosalie, who was riding on Flatorte to Laika's side. The ghost was full-on shaking.
"Why are *you* scared, Rosalie?!"

"I'd lose my entire identity if I was brought back to life…"

"That's an awfully human concern."

"And if that happened, I wouldn't be able to float or pass through walls anymore…"

"I guess from a ghost's perspective, you'd just be reverting to a less convenient lifestyle."

No one thing could make everyone happy, it seemed.

"Gosh, I would be delighted if she's devised some sort of new alcoholic beverage! I've heard you can make some really unusual drinks by fermenting fruits from the south!"

Halkara was the same as always. But her suggestion seemed a lot more likely. And if that's all it was, at least there wouldn't be too much trouble involved.

And so we arrived at the kingdom of the dead, Thursa Thursa, without issue.

Muu and Nahna Nahna were waiting for us when we got there.

"Oi, good to see ya. I'll take ya straight there. Come right 'is way, just follow me………………… Ughhh……… I'm already knackered…"

Muu turned and attempted to walk, but she immediately exhausted herself.

"Did you really think that was going to work?"

"Oof… Guess I'll walk an' talk… This was a type o' café 'at was once real popular in the old days o' the Thursa Thursa Kingdom… Urgh! Come on, move it! Once I make me first step, I swear I'll get the next one…!"

"I have a feeling you'll finish explaining long before we get there, so feel free to wait."

In the end, Muu used her ghost powers to move her body.

On the way to our destination, I tried to figure out what the secret was based on what Muu had said.

A type of café that was popular in the ancient days… Was this going to be like the maid café again…?

It was better not to get too hung up on the word *ancient*. The civilization Muu had lived in was extremely advanced. It had probably had almost anything I could think of.

Furthermore, Nahna Nahna's outfit looked a bit like a maid's dress... If people in outfits like hers would be doing the serving, it'd be a maid café by default.

But it would be tactless of me if I said as much and ended up being right, so I decided to stay silent.

Muu and Rosalie were chatting in front of me.

"Di'n't wanna wait too long. I 'ad a good number, an' they're tame enough, so I figured it's time."

"Tame? What do you mean?"

"You'll see. There's a gate ahead, yeah? The café's just past it. Use any free table ya like."

Just as she said, beyond an arched wooden gate was a series of tables and chairs. And all around...were cats!

I could see black cats, orange tabbies, and ones with ears flat against their heads like Scottish folds! There were even some that looked like mousy-gray British shorthairs! Wait, wasn't it a little odd to describe a cat as "mousy"?

"Well? Whaddaya think? These sorts o' cat cafés was popular back in the old civ. You can play wiv cats while ya relax. Great idea, ey?"

Muu seemed proud of herself as she told us about it.

I see... When she said "tame," she was talking about the cat staff (?) members.

I could hear the children cheering from behind me. Falfa was the first to rush forward, and Shalsha followed right behind her. They immediately took their seats and reached out to pet the cats' heads.

"They're so cuuuute! These kitties are adorable!"

"I see most of them are southern varieties. Not many have long hair. But all cat breeds are cute."

In my opinion, the cutest thing was the girls playing with the cats. It was such a lovely sight. I would definitely have been taking pictures and posting them on Instagram if this world had such a thing.

"You're an obsessed parent, Azusa. They're just petting cats," Sandra said flatly as more of the animals quickly gathered around her. "Hey, come on, what's with you? I thought cats were carnivores. Sheesh, you want pets? Fine, I'll give you pets."

Sandra didn't look as displeased as she sounded. I guess everyone found cats charming.

"This is a great idea, Muu!" I said. "Just fantastic! It's definitely your best idea so far!"

"What's wrong with the ones before, eh…?"

Muu looked at me with a strange expression, but if you asked me, cooling down the entire ancient civilization wasn't just weird, it was a whole lot of trouble.

"The ghosts o' the kingdom use'ta keep cats to pass the time. An' I thought, 'ey, why not start up a cat café? An' that's 'ow all 'is came about."

It was totally worth coming all this way.

"All right, everyone. Take your seats, and we'll—"

I stopped.

Laika's eyes were sparkling.

She must *really* love cats. I didn't have to ask—I could see it in her face.

Come to think of it, most people had the impression that the more serious-minded a person was, the fonder they were of the free-spirited cat. This was just a myth, however. Lazy people weren't suited to take care of pets, period, and that went for both dogs *and* cats.

Flatorte, meanwhile, was locked in a staring contest with a brown cat.

"You wanna fight with me, the great Flatorte?! You sure have guts!"

"No sparring with the cats!"

This was a café, so there was a menu. I asked the ghost waiter to give me the menu for the living, but—

"Then I guess we'll all have boiled well water."

—since this was the land of the dead, there wasn't a lot to choose from.

"There's food, too, y'know. Why don't ya try some? The Black-Green Moor o' the Dead's a whole set."

Muu poked at the menu.

"This isn't the type of café a person orders a set meal at," I said.

The picture she was pointing at looked like an *okonomiyaki* set.

The Black-Green Moor of the Dead seemed to be an ancient dish that kind of resembled *okonomiyaki*. Maybe it came down to cultural difference, but I wish it sounded a little yummier.

"Ya know I went out of me way to make sure the livin' people had a menu, too. There's even a sauce noodles set."

I'd never heard of sauce noodles before, but it sounded like *yakisoba*.

"I'll order one of those next time we stop by."

To reiterate, this was not the type of café one came to for eating. The main point of this place was to play with the cats.

Laika, in particular, was now rolling around on the floor as the kitties crawled all over her.

"Ah-ha-ha-ha~ That tickles! You are kind of heavy, aren't you? Ha-ha-ha, ha-ha-ha~"

"Laika's expression is so soft… All her tension has vanished…"

I was glad she was having fun, but I had no idea she'd be so into this…

"Oh, I see you are getting closer to my face. Is there something on it? Ha-ha-ha~ My, have you decided to sleep on my tummy? Am I warm? Ha-ha-ha~"

Laika looked like she was going to melt… I bet she'd be willing to come to the Thursa Thursa Kingdom just to visit this place.

Flatorte, on the other hand, was looking very suave, drinking her well water at the table. It wasn't a very suave drink, but it *was* literally the only thing on the menu.

"Mistress, Laika is much too soft. She usually acts so stoic, but once she's surrounded by cats, she loses herself. Unless she gets her act together, she'll never be the strongest."

"Uh, I don't think fawning over cats is much of an issue, but…yeah, I suppose Laika is acting pretty different right now."

Laika wore a look of pure bliss as the cats surrounded her. My daughters were playing with them, too, but Laika was far and away the one having the best time.

"I 'ad no idea it'd be such a big 'it wiv the dragon girl."

A kitten was sprawled over Muu's head. I wasn't sure if the cat had climbed up her or if she had put it there.

"Thanks for all this, Muu. Everyone's having a great time."

"Cats were valuable creatures 'ere in the kingdom. We use'ta run cat cafés like 'is one in order to keep large numbers of 'em. There are probably about three 'undred cats an' their relatives just at this café."

"Hmm? Cat relatives? Does that you mean you have animals other than housecats?"

At that moment, Halkara screamed.

"Eeeeeeeeeeeek! Stopppppppp!"

I looked over to see Halkara in a lion's mouth with only her face sticking out.

"Sh-she's being eaten! This is bad!"

"Oh, 'at's just Corozawan the lion. It's fine. He's just playin'. He won't eat 'er."

Muu gave the lion's name without a second thought. This must have been what she meant by cat relatives.

"It doesn't look all that fine to me!"

"Ya know 'ow cats lick people's 'ands, yeah? This is the same thing. He's trained."

But Halkara was going pale.

"Ooh… It's so slimy… So warm and gross… I feel like a helpless prey animal…"

"We worshipped the cat's relatives as divine creatures, see. Seein' 'em makes ya remember just how small we all are."

I had a feeling it was more about physical size than divinity.

Just then, a tiger sauntered over and licked Halkara's face.

"Wah! Its tongue is so rough! Rougher than I thought it'd be! Why are only the big animals coming to me?!"

"That's Arkey the tiger. A long time ago, we used to 'ave a round shrine dedica'ed to the tiger god. It's all covered in vines now, though."

"I'm a little more concerned about Halkara than historical facts right now. Are you *really* sure she's all right?"

"Sheesh! Insistent, aren'cha? We've trained 'em not to eat anyone! But—I suppose animals *do* understand power hierarchies very quickly."

Muu nodded sagely.

"So is Halkara in danger or not…?"

Just then, Nahna Nahna arrived with another round of well water.

"Please take a look at the space around you and Flatorte."

I did as she asked, but I didn't see anything different. However, when I looked a little farther away, I saw lions, tigers, and leopards staring toward us in fear.

"Huh. What did I do…?"

"Animals can tell instinctively if you're the sort of person who will play with them. For example, they know that if they pick Flatorte up with their mouths, she will fight back."

"Of course I will. I won't let them get away with licking my face! I don't care if it's a lion or a tiger—they *will* be punished!" Flatorte exclaimed with feeling.

"Some of the larger cats may want to fawn over Miss Laika, but then the smaller cats would run away, which would put Miss Laika in a bad mood. Thus, they cannot approach her, either."

I understood the ghost's explanation, but—

"I guess that means Halkara's licked."

"Nice one, Azusa. Nahna Nahna, another glass o' well water for Azusa."

At least give me a real drink.

When Halkara was eventually freed from the lion's mouth, she looked a little—no, *very* exhausted.

"Ah… I'm drenched… Predators are terrifying…"

Halkara came to lie down next Laika, who was still playing with the cats on the floor.

"You sure had a rough time there, Halkara…"

"Oh, do you think lion or tiger spit could be sold as a potion? It must be very difficult to obtain, so I could probably sell it at a premium!"

Apparently, Halkara wasn't going to overlook *any* opportunity to turn a profit.

With that matter settled, a thought suddenly crossed my mind.

"I haven't seen Rosalie for a while. Does she not like cats?"

Maybe ghosts couldn't play with living cats—no, that couldn't be right. If that were true, how could a country full of ghosts collect enough cats for a café? In fact, what would even be the point?

"What're you on about? Rosalie's playin' just above us."

Muu pointed skyward. And there she was, moving around with great delight.

"Eh-hee-hee-hee! That tickles! Stop, stop!"

"Huh? What are you doing up there all by yourself, Rosalie?"

"Playing with ghost cats."

"There are ghost cats?!"

Now that I thought about it, it made sense that the souls of animals might occasionally remain in this world, too. In fact, the ghosts here were probably particularly interested in looking after ghost cats.

"Cats 'ave their regrets, too. We take care of 'em, both livin' an' dead."

"That's very admirable of you."

As I was having this conversation, a little cat leaped up onto Flatorte's lap.

"Do you not fear for your life? Hmm. I applaud your bravery."

She cuddled the small creature—Flatorte didn't hate cats, either.

Halkara was enjoying herself, too. She had a kitten riding on her shoulder.

"It's a lot more comfortable to have a cat riding on me than for me to ride on a lion!"

I wasn't sure if what had happened to Halkara constituted "riding on a lion."

From that point on, lots of kittens started to gather around her. Apparently, there was something about Halkara that attracted baby cats in particular.

Laika looked jealous.

"It seems they think of Miss Halkara as a fellow kitten friend," she said.

Perhaps the lion had put her in its mouth to protect her...

Presently, the same lion started walking around the café with my three girls on its back.

"This is fuuun! It's like riding a horse~!"

"In a far-off land, there is a story about a man who rode a tiger. He knew that as soon as he alighted from the creature, he would be eaten. The story is supposed to illustrate a situation where one must forget minor details and push forward."

"Riding an animal makes me feel as though the plants have won. It's a very nice feeling."

Their reactions were a little different from a normal child's, but they were having fun, and that's what counted.

"You put together a menu for us, even though we're the only human customers you have," I said. "Sorry for making you go through all the trouble."

Muu was corporeal, but she still didn't drink anything, and the other people of her kingdom did not have physical bodies at all. They had no need for cafés.

"Ah, you're wrong, but I 'preciate it. We 'ave a corporeal regular already. I wouldn't put together a menu just for you lot. She'll be 'ere any second now, actually."

"Oh, that's right. Demons visit, too, these days, don't they?"

"Yeah, but this one's a li'l different."

"Different from the demons…?"

"Yep. She's been comin' ev'ry day since we opened."

Muu's gaze drifted to the gate at the café entrance.

"Ah, there she is."

A little ways away, at the entrance, stood a huge ball of hair.

"That's—That's Ost Ande!"

I'd never mistake her strange form. It was Ost Ande, the reaper.

Hands slunk out of the hair and pulled apart one section to reveal her face. It *was* her.

"…Hello," she said. "What a coincidence."

"I suppose it is… I didn't know you ever left the Empty Wastes…"

"…This is a special place," she said. She then took her spot in an empty chair and started petting a cat on the table. "…Literary scholars work at cafés… And they like cats."

That had to be some kind of stereotype…

"Oh, you know 'er, Azusa?" asked Muu. "Yeah, I thought she was kinda weird."

"No need to be rude. But she *is* exceptionally strange. You didn't think anything of it?"

She'd cause a panic if she appeared in a human city.

"I got a strange feelin' off 'er, since I couldn't tell if she was livin' or dead. But some customers are just like that, y'know? Business is business, don't matter who's payin'."

It was true that it would be impossible to tell if a god like Ost Ande was alive or dead, and maybe to Muu, the divide between living and dead was more important than that between human and demon or whatnot.

"Well, I guess it's fine, so long as there aren't any problems."

There was no need for me to expose her as a god, and if she wanted to, she would say so herself.

"Lady Azusa, you know that hairy person?" Laika asked me from the floor, but her face was covered in cats, so I couldn't see her. She was really spoiling those animals.

Now that I thought about it, none of the family knew about Ost Ande. This would be a great opportunity to tell them, but I had no idea if it was all right for me to tell them about her divinity...

I asked Ost Ande in a whisper, "Hey, you don't mind if I tell them what you actually are, do you?"

"...Do as you like. I've led an embarrassing life, but it's nothing worth hiding."

I had her permission, so I told the family and Muu that she was the reaper.

Shalsha was intensely interested and asked Ost Ande all sorts of questions, but that was all that happened. This was a world of demons and spirits, after all.

"Huh. So she was a reaper. She did look the part," Muu murmured, watching as Ost Ande sat with a cat in her arms and answered Shalsha's questions.

"It looks like that doesn't bother you at all, Muu. You're not scared of her as a spirit?"

"The reaper deals in freshly escaped souls. She's got nuffin to do wiv us; we've been dead for ages."

That meant I wouldn't need to negotiate a peace between the spirits and the reaper.

"Actually, why don't ya ask 'er yerself. Go join the Q&A wiv Shalsha."

Muu was right. I brought over a chair and sat beside Shalsha.

"So, Reaper, do you not capture the souls of this world?"

"...Correct. By remaining, spirits maintain the balance. It is not good for too many to leave this plane."

I see, I see. Ghosts are normal, then.

"...Though I don't capture spirits, I can still see them. Like this."

Ost Ande's tendril-like hands reached out into empty space.

"...There is a ghost cat here. There are many, in fact, since this is the land of ghosts."

"I see. I bet they like having a lot of friends around."

At that moment, her tendril hand began to shudder.

"...Oh. It's going wild. Really wild."

We couldn't see anything, so it was hard to tell, but I had a feeling I knew what was happening.

"You're wrapping your arm around the cat, right? Even a ghost would put up some resistance..."

"...No. It is reacting to the presence of a string-like object and playing with it."

"I guess cats are still cats, even in the afterlife."

Some things never changed...

"...The ghost may only be playing, but it *is* getting a bit excited. It has a lot of energy."

Again, very catlike. It's probably getting more and more into playing with the string.

Ost Ande's tendril was jumping all over the place. It looked like she had her hands full.

"...Calm yourself. It's not good for a spirit to lose control."

There was something ominous in what she said. Coming from the reaper, however, anything could start sounding scary. It was too easy to read into her words.

"What do you mean 'not good'? Will its soul fall apart or something?"

"...No. With an excess of vigor, a spirit may gain the ability to enter into things it usually cannot."

In the next moment—

—I felt something hit my head!

"Whoa! What was that?!"

It was a lot like walking down a path and suddenly being blindsided by a flying ball. It didn't hurt, but I could feel my whole brain shudder.

I toppled over backward, chair and all. There was no pain, but I sure was surprised.

"...I am sorry. The cat spirit jumped away from me and...crashed into you."

"Spirits can do that...?"

I stood, holding my head. Shalsha extended a hand to help me up and asked, "Mom, are you okay...?"

I still felt dizzy. "Thanks, Shalsha. I'm not hurt, so don't worry. I'm fine."

"...Both ghosts and living beings have souls. The souls rarely interact, but one can sometimes slam into another when it gets overexcited."

From what Ost Ande said, it seemed the cat ghost had started rushing around and bumped into my own soul.

"So the overexcited ghost cat just happened to fly right at me. I get it."

"...As the reaper, I was not strict enough with the spirit... I apologize. How embarrassing. I wish to crawl under a rock."

Ost Ande hid her face behind her hair again. She was extremely humble for a god.

"I'm not angry, so you don't have to hide yourself. It's not your fault anyway—it's the cat's fault."

I *could* say it was the tendril's fault, but she hadn't intended to excite the cat, so there was no use placing blame.

"...It's still my fault. I was not paying enough attention." Ost Ande's voice filtered out from the ball of hair.

"No, no, it really isn't your fault, Ost Ande. I'm not even hurt." I still had my hand to my head, but there wasn't even a bump.

"...That may be so, but injury is not the only issue."

She was really being down on herself, and I was starting to feel bad.

"It isn't your fault, Ost Ande, really! You can come out now! As they say, hate the sin, not the reaper!"

"...I thank you deeply for your kindness."

Ost Ande's face finally appeared from behind all the hair. I had no idea she was such a stickler for politeness. Personally, I thought she was a little *too* polite.

My head had stopped spinning, so I took my hand off it.

And then—

"Oh."

Shalsha looked surprised.

"What? I'm sure I wasn't injured. Did I get a leaf in my hair when I fell?"

I'd been saddled with all manner of odd jobs ever since reaching max level, but one thing I was grateful for was that my body was way sturdier now.

"Mom... **You've got way bigger problems than a leaf in your hair**...," Shalsha said. Her voice was grave, but her lips were twisted into a little smile.

What did she mean?

"Be more specific, please. You're worrying me."

"Mom, put your hand on your head again."

I did as she said, and I felt something soft.

From behind me, I heard Muu say, "Here, take a gander." She was holding out a hand mirror.

I took it and looked at myself.

I had cat ears on my head.

"Gaaaaaaah! What's happeniiiiiing?!"

The other family members came rushing over at my voice.

"Wah! Mommy, you're a kitty! You're so cute!"

Falfa hugged me. Okay, that was nice, but this wasn't the time for that.

Halkara nodded and said, "Oh, Madam Teacher, I didn't know you were a furry." *Stop. Stop acting like you understand me.*

Sandra gently withdrew with an "Ugh." *Ouch, that really stings.*

Flatorte calmly said, "Hey, that's new." *Flatorte, this is not normal!*

"Oh, the cat soul's inside you," Rosalie commented, offering a concrete analysis of the situation. Now I was really worried.

The most intense reaction came from Laika. At first, she just silently stared.

"L-Lady Azusa... Y-you're...you're so cute... You're so...um...so cute...it hurts...," she whispered, covering her reddening face with her hands.

"Why does it hurt? What does that mean?"

"I-it means you're s-so cute that I can feel my heart constricting..."

Should I be happy about that? I wasn't sure...

"And now I see I have a cat tail, too! What on earth is going on?!"

My eyes locked with Ost Ande's.

"...I am relieved to hear that you don't mind."

Oh, so Ost Ande knew this was going to happen. *That's* why she was so apologetic...

"Actually, I meant I didn't mind you flinging the cat into me. This situation is a whole other matter..."

"...Um... Okay... See you later." Ost Ande tried to slowly retreat into her ball of hair, but I tore it open.

"Don't run! Tell me how to solve this!"

"...I'll pay you damages."

"No! I want a *solution*, not compensation!"

I needed her to tell me how to fix this... But for some reason, my attention kept being drawn to strange things.

One of Ost Ande's hairs started swaying, and I suddenly struck out with my hand to bat at it.

"My body is moving on its own!"

As if driven by some feline instinct, I felt the urge to smack anything waving around in front of me.

Next, I spotted Flatorte's tail swishing back and forth.

"Mraow!" I pounced and grabbed hold of it. "I did it again!"

"If you're going to go after my tail, Mistress, at least warn me. Attacking another's tail without prior warning is against the rules."

I wasn't attacking it—it was just instinct…

And then, when I turned my attention upward, I saw several transparent cats floating above me…

The ghost cats… There were way more of them than I'd thought. Now that the cat's soul was inside me, I could see them…

"I was only away for a moment, but I see things have taken an amusing turn."

The surprisingly calm voice came from Nahna Nahna, who had returned with my drink.

"This isn't amusing at all," I said.

"We are experts when it comes to matters of the soul, so you may consult with us."

Maybe it was a good idea to rely on Nahna Nahna and the other ghosts for this.

Ost Ande was avoiding my gaze, after all. I bet she had no idea how to solve this.

"…If I simply sit down and write an essay on a subject I am not an expert in, I will only be humiliated later. It is safer not to speak of things with which I am unfamiliar."

I found it a little strange that the reaper was not an "expert" on matters of the soul. This seemed like a rare case, however, so maybe that was why she didn't know.

"Miss Nahna Nahna, will you help me?"

"I notice you don't meow during normal speech."

Suddenly, relying on her was a less attractive prospect…

We were taken to Nahna Nahna's house (which was, to be more precise, a large tomb). The inside was an open cavern—a good place for our meeting. It was damp and moldy, but that wasn't a problem for the ghosts.

"It seems the soul of a cat has entered Azusa's body. Cases like this occur from time to time." Nahna Nahna spoke impersonally, but the professionalism made her sound more reliable.

"While you look like a catperson on the outside right now, your soul is something entirely different. A catperson has only one soul—the soul of the catperson. Inside Azusa, however, there is both her own soul and the soul of the cat."

I see.

"Which means if we extract the cat's soul, she will return to normal. We will simply be taking one away."

I nodded. "Oh yeah, like when Rosalie entered Halkara's body in the past."

"What an awful memory…" Halkara went pale. She'd been through a lot back then…

"But I thought my soul was too powerful for her to enter."

I was pretty sure the reason Rosalie chose Halkara's body was because she couldn't enter mine. It was a bit rude toward Halkara, but Beelzebub said that those with irresponsible personalities were easier to enter.

"Well, it's deep in there, so the usual defenses ain't workin'," said Muu. "It's like you've got fick walls, see, but it's already in the city 'avin' a grand old time."

"Yeah, okay."

Walls and moats were defenses meant to keep invaders out, but they weren't very effective against those already inside.

"Should be easy, innit. We just needa chase the cat's soul out. If it wanted to leave, it could go anytime. Dunna, though. Wa'eva, innit."

"Muu, this is the one time I don't want to hear you say you don't know…"

Muu stared hard at my face. No—I had a feeling she was looking at something deeper inside.

"I knew it," she said.

"You knew what?"

"The kitty says it don't wanna leave."

"It doesn't want to leave? Why?! My own soul is in there, too! How can it relax?"

Maybe the cat was a bit of an eccentric, and I'd just gotten unlucky.

"Might be 'ard for a livin' person to tell, but your soul is warm, Azusa. For a cat, it must be right cozy. Livin' cats like warm places, yeah? Same fing."

"Oh no…"

I pictured a cat that didn't want to leave its spot by the radiator.

Muu then turned to Ost Ande. "You're the reaper, yeah? Don'cha know 'ow to fix this? You're the expert 'ere."

"…I can manage free-roaming souls. But…peeling a spirit away from a living creature…will cause harm."

Another ominous line from the reaper…

"…In the worst-case scenario, Azusa will die. If a reaper has chosen a soul to capture, that is not a problem, but this is different… If she dies because I made a mistake, then I will be liable."

"Oh, then please don't do that," I said.

It sounded terrifying.

"Miss Azusa." For some reason, Nahna Nahna was smiling. I didn't know she could do that. It was a rare sight. "You must give up," she said.

"No! It's too early to give up! And didn't you say you were an expert? You *just* said that!"

"It is precisely because I am an expert that I will not offer baseless statements to soothe your conscience."

That might seem like a sound argument, but in this situation, I was sure it was just an excuse.

"It's not as though you are being inconvenienced. Your soul is preserved, and the cat is simply staying with you for a while. It shouldn't tire you out mentally or physically, either."

"But I have cat ears and a tail!"

"That's hardly a problem. Your words and actions may become more catlike, as well, but that is all."

Nahna Nahna held out a plant. It was a stem of foxtail or something similar. She waved the stem around like it was a cat toy.

Fsh, fsh, fsh!

*That's the sound of me batting at the foxtail.

"Gah! It's happening again!"

"Sometimes, the feline instinct will come to the forefront like this, but you will become accustomed to it in no time."

"I don't want to get accustomed to it! There's a *cat* in here with me, you know! I think this counts as an exceptional circumsta—"

Nahna Nahna shook the foxtail again.

Fsh, fsh, fsh!

Once again, I pawed (?) at it.

"Dammit! I try not to react, but my body keeps moving on its own!"

"I get it, Mistress. Sometimes I get so angry I can't stop myself."

"I'm pretty sure that's not the same, Flatorte."

Blue dragons were just quick to pick fights.

"And it seems to be popular with a few members of your family," said Nahna Nahna.

Falfa's and Shalsha's eyes were sparkling. Laika's face was beet red. If anything, this only made me feel even more embarrassed.

"Um...I'm very sorry, but I don't intend to stay like this..."

"Falfa likes you this way, too, Mommy~"

"Even if you turn into a cat, Sis and I will take care of you, Mom."

My daughters did not seem to understand my plight.

"I...um...I can't calm down, so I would appreciate it if you could return to normal...," said Laika. "If this continues, I will be unable to face my training with a clear mind..."

At least Laika wanted me to turn back. But what did she mean by "unable to face her training with a clear mind"...?

Ost Ande said, "...If you'll excuse me," and tried to leave, so I grabbed one of her tendrils and stopped her. I needed her to stay a little longer. But if even she didn't know how to eject the cat soul from my body, then there wasn't much more we could do.

"Well, we could **coax the cat soul out**."

"*Sigh*... I guess I'll live my life with cat ears for a little while... I'll need to wear my hat all the time so that Beelzebub doesn't laugh at me when she visits... But I can't hide the tail— What?"

I rushed over to Muu and grabbed her by the shoulders.

"There's a way? There's a way?!"

"Calm down, calm down! Yeah, but it'll take a whole fortnight!"

What on earth kind of process would take two weeks?

"The cat god festival will be takin' place 'ere in the Thursa Thursa Kingdom in two weeks' time. All the ghost cats will get togevah as part o' the celebration."

I guess the ancient civilization really did worship cats as gods.

"And that kitty inside ya won't be able to resist the festival. Basically, if anyfin' attracts its attention more'n you, it'll leave."

"So I've gotta wait until the festival..."

Two weeks. That was an odd chunk of time. I had a feeling Beelzebub might show up at least twice... That said, I didn't think I'd be able to come up with a way to get the cat to leave on my own.

"Fine... I'll wait for the cat god festival."

Desperate situations called for desperate measures.

"Then it's settled—" Nahna Nahna's hand came to rest on Muu's shoulder.

"—Your Majesty, this is the perfect opportunity to bleed her dry."

"I don't think a minister should be saying things like that," I pointed out. She was definitely plotting something.

"No need to worry. It's not scary, and it won't even hurt."

Whenever Nahna Nahna told me not to worry, I couldn't help getting nervous...

"I guess there's nothing I can do for now..."

My head drooped. So did my new tail.

"...And now. If you'll excuse me." Ost Ande left, still refusing to meet my gaze.

I sensed that she was ready to do anything to avoid getting involved...

Afterward, the whole family went back to the house in the highlands, and we resumed our daily routine.

"Hi, everyone! G'morning!"

"It's so strange to see you wearing your hat at breakfast, Madam Teacher...," Halkara pointed out right away.

"It's because I have cat ears..."

Reluctantly, I decided to remove my hat going forward.

It didn't seem like the ghost cat had any plans to act recklessly, so at least on the surface, everything was normal. The main differences were the cat ears and tail.

But even that proved to be a huge problem.

"I'm here~!"

Just as I was killing some nearby slimes, I ran into Beelzebub, who was walking toward the house from Flatta.

She's here already.

"O-oh, um, hi... It's me, normal Azusa..."

"............"

A brief, awkward silence settled between us.

"......Gah! What is this? I'd no idea you were into that sort of thing!"

"I'm not *into* anything! There's a very complicated reason for all of this! Actually...I suppose it's not that complicated, really."

I explained the whole thing to her. As a result, I ended up telling Beelzebub about the reaper, too, but it was probably fine.

"And that is why you are living as a catperson, hmm? You are quite a magnet for trouble. Almost as much as Halkara is."

"I think Halkara has it much worse. And you're not one to talk, since Pecora's always getting you wrapped up in things, too. Pot, kettle."

"'Tis simply my boss's nature. It has nothing to do with my own disposition. In fact, perhaps I should tell Her Majesty about—"

"Not a word to her."

I quickly cut Beelzebub off. I didn't even need to consider it.

"Very well. I pity you, so I shan't say a word of this to Her Majesty. Be grate—"

"Mraaaooow!"

I leaped into the air and swiped at a slime.

"...Why must you interrupt me in this manner?"

"Ah-ha-ha-ha... I can't stop jumping at things that move."

Ever since I'd sprouted these cat ears, I felt like my reflexes when I attacked slimes had gotten better.

"If you want to learn more about the catperson lifestyle, I can ask Pondeli for you."

"No! I'm not trying to live like a catperson. Though I appreciate the sentiment."

"And if you're looking to move to the town around Vanzeld Castle, I can provide you with your choice of property."

"I'm not moving!"

It seemed that to Beelzebub, the cat ears made me look like a demon.

I found I had some new problems thanks to my temporary feline nature.

For instance, when we were having stew for dinner, I spent most of my time blowing on it to cool it down.

"It isn't all that hot, Mistress. I don't like hot things, either, so I made it a nice temperature."

Flatorte had made dinner that day, and the soup bowl was stuffed full of ingredients. Flatorte always made hearty dishes when she cooked.

"But it still feels hot... I'll eat it once it cools."

Now that I had a cat's tongue, I had a newfound aversion to anything giving off steam.

And that wasn't the only thing that made me aware of my catlike qualities. I'd started wanting to avoid baths as well.

I was sitting in my room thinking, *I'm not that dirty. Maybe I can skip it this time...*

I shook my head.

"No! I can't compromise like this! I'm forcing myself in! Some cats like taking baths—I shouldn't generalize!"

Aside from my occasional reflexive reactions, I had complete control over my body, and I was able to get in the bath. Still, I spent way less time in the water than usual.

"I can't even relax while I'm soaking..."

There was a voice inside me screaming at me to get out. Being part cat sure was difficult...

I also opted out of going shopping in Flatta. If even one of the villagers spotted me, it'd spread through the whole place like wildfire. They loved gossip, after all.

Thankfully, the other family members switched shopping days with me, so I managed to avoid it.

The two weeks passed—they had felt both long and short at the same time.

At last, I left for the Thursa Thursa Kingdom's cat god festival.

I couldn't imagine how awful it would be if I was late and had to wait another year, so I gave myself plenty of time to get there flying on Laika's back.

"*Sigh*, I suppose this marks the end of your cat life, Lady Azusa."

"Why do you sound so disappointed...?"

"Personally, I...would rather like it if you could become part cat for about one day each month..."

"N-no thanks!"

I wasn't going to do that—not even for Laika.

◇

When we arrived at the Thursa Thursa Kingdom, it was decorated in all kinds of banners and flags. It really felt like a festival was about to start.

Muu and Nahna Nahna came to greet us right away.

"There ya are. You're the star o' this year's festival. Ya need to rehearse."

"Okay... I'll do anything to get back to normal."

Muu said I needed to "rehearse," but I was essentially just a decoration, so it was pretty easy.

The cat god festival was a celebration that honored a humanoid cat deity the people of the ancient Thursa Thursa Kingdom once fervently worshipped. This time, I'd been chosen to play the part of cat god. Apparently, the festival had an even greater impact when the one chosen had actual cat ears.

First, I got on the palanquin, and we practiced marching down the chosen route. I thought I wouldn't have to do anything, since I was just riding, but there were some spots where I was supposed to shout in a loud voice.

Then, at the climax of the festival, I had to deliver an oracle as the god, so I had to memorize a very long passage. That was probably the most difficult part.

"Can't I put a little cheat sheet on the floor or something?" I asked Nahna Nahna, who was acting as my instructor.

"Miss Azusa, this is a very important celebration for us. I would appreciate it if you took this seriously. You must respect other cultures."

"Ugh... You're right... I can't argue with that."

This was a traditional festival. I couldn't cut corners here.

I did eventually manage to memorize my lines, but that wasn't the end. If anything, that was just the beginning.

"Good. Now try and recite the lines with inflection."

"Ugh... You mean I have to make it like a performance?"

"Of course you do. This is an important ceremony. We can't have you speaking in a monotone. That would spoil the whole event. You must convince the people that you are truly the cat god."

Once again, she was right, and I couldn't argue.

"It is important to repeat these lines several times over. Now begin again from the top."

"Uh, okay... Meow, I'm the cat god..."

"You're too quiet! You are playing the part of divinity! Act like it!"

"Hrrrgh! You're so strict!"

Nevertheless, I survived Nahna Nahna's very rigorous instruction. She was right. I was the star of this performance. I wanted to touch everyone's hearts! And then I wanted to be freed from this cat hell!

"Very good. I see the sparkle in your eyes. Now let us run through it one more time."

"Yes! Let's do it! I'll play the part of the cat god perfectly! No, I will *become* the god!"

And then at last, the day of the cat god festival was upon us.

I stepped from the ruins that enshrined the cat god, got onto the palanquin held aloft by ghosts, and rode as they marched along the chosen route.

As the cat god, I wore a bright and colorful costume.

All the guests were from the Thursa Thursa Kingdom, so there shouldn't be any rumors. There was no risk, so I was going to go full steam ahead.

The palanquin set off, and I saw more ghosts than I had ever seen in my life. Had they all taken corporeal forms at once?

No. Because I had a cat spirit inside me, I could see all the ghostly spectators with my own eyes. It seemed the Thursa Thursa Kingdom was alive and well, so to speak. The streets were thronging.

I turned to the crowd and waved.

I could hear a lot of people shouting, "Cat God, Cat God!"

You know, this wasn't so bad. I was kind of enjoying it. Even though I had been forced into this role against my will, it genuinely made me happy to be doing something for someone else.

The palanquin reached a turn. I had to say a line here.

I struck a pose and made my fingers into claws.

"Meow, I'm the cat god! Praise me more, meow!"

I couldn't let myself feel embarrassed. If I were really the cat god, I would feel no shame doing this.

But off in the distance, I could see a table and chair. *That must be a guest of honor.*

And there, in the chair, sat Pecora.

No! This is bad...

"P...praise...me... Meow..."

My voice suddenly went quiet.

One of the ghosts carrying the palanquin said, "Try to be a little louder." *Yeah, I know.*

But...

Pecora was here! As a guest of honor!

I'd slipped up. The Thursa Thursa Kingdom had ties to the demons. It was natural for Pecora to be invited to such an event.

And it was already too late—Pecora was leaning way over, staring straight at me!

"Oh, the one playing the part of the god looks a lot like my elder sister... Hmm? Hmmmm?"

Maybe she hadn't noticed yet. Or could she already tell who I was? Either way, I had a feeling I was done for.

After that, I shouted, "Meow, I'm the cat god! Praise me more, meow! Give me gifts! Meeeooow!" just as I was supposed to do. And each time I did, I noticed Pecora following me at a distance.

Stay in your seat, woman!

But judging by her expression, it didn't seem like she was plotting anything. She was simply peering at me suspiciously. Perhaps she still hadn't discarded the possibility that this was just a chance likeness.

The festival clothes probably helped. I must look very different.

Oh, and it was only now that I realized my tail was waving back and forth. Maybe she saw me as an actual catperson. If I were just wearing a costume, the attached tail wouldn't move around like this.

It seemed like Beelzebub hadn't told Pecora about my cat situation. I was really thankful she'd kept her promise.

"Right. I'm going to put on my best act until this festival is over."

I was going to get through this. I would show them all what the Witch of the Highlands could do!

—Oh, right, I wasn't supposed to be the Witch of the Highlands… I was the cat god. No one else. I had nothing to do with Azusa or any witches!

"Meow, I'm the cat god! Watch out, meow! Some flowers are poisonous for cats!"

The ghosts carrying the palanquin said, "Your performance has gotten much better. Keep it up!" I'd made a breakthrough.

I wasn't even acting anymore. I *was* a catperson. Pecora could follow the parade with that unsatisfied look on her face all she liked! In fact, I didn't even know who Pecora was! To me, she was just a guest of honor—some important stranger!

After I had meowed in several designated spots along the way, the palanquin reached its final destination—Muu's grave (which was also a shrine and her house).

Her grave was also a large structure somewhat like a pyramid, so it wasn't especially spooky.

We wouldn't be going inside. The palanquin was carried along the outer stairs to about halfway up the grave. A spacious temporary stage had been built there. From it, I could see out over the entire kingdom.

The final part of the program would take place here.

Muu emerged from the grave and took a seat on my palanquin.

Even Muu, the queen, had to humble herself before the god, so she dipped her head.

"Mind not your manners, meow. Lift your head, meow."

Muu did as instructed.

"Ha-ha, Cat God. It's been a while! The Thursa Thursa Kingdom is thrivin' fanks to you! I wanna keep it up, so lend us a paw in the comin' years, ey?"

Perhaps because the divine parlance sounded so much like a cockney accent, I couldn't sense a hint of regal dignity in her words. But it wasn't like the cat god could point any of that out. I had to stick to the script.

"I'm impressed, meow. You speak the divine parlance with ease, meow!"

This was not my personal opinion. I was merely reciting the script.

"But if you want my help, show me more, more of your faith, meow!"

I sounded really arrogant, but again, this was all in the script.

"We've prepared several sideshows just for yer entertainment, Cat God! First, a race!"

I then heard a loud cheer in the distance, and I looked down to the ground from the stage.

Several ghosts who apparently had been good at athletics in life began to run (?). It looked like their feet were touching the ground, at least.

"Run, run, run! Everyone in fifth place an' above gets prize moneeey!"

The idea was to entertain the cat god with some running around.

"The view's pretty good from 'ere, innit? You've got the perfect spot!"

Muu had scarcely taken part in any of the practices, but she was

We Went to a Cat Café 117

basically acting the same as always, so I guess she didn't need to. With a real queen taking the role of the sovereign, there wasn't much she had to do differently.

"Yes, meow. I have a great view, meow."

"There're several turns along the course, an' some people tend to fall. See? That one's already eatin' dirt."

I guess ghosts could fall over, too.

"This is a dangerous sport, meow…"

"This use'ta take place in the temple. I 'eard it was started in the era of Epise the Third."

"It has quite the history, meow."

After about a minute, the top contenders reached the goal, and the race was over.

"That was nice, Queen, meow. But it was too simple—not interesting enough, meow!"

We had only been watching some people run around, after all.

"Gotcha. Then I 'ope you will enjoy watchin' the float fight."

Floats, each well over nine meters long, appeared from all corners of the kingdom. They started drifting towards each other on a collision course.

"Yaaah!" "Don't lose to the next town over!" "Smash 'em!"

When they collided, the floats would shudder, sometimes even toppling over.

"This is getting real violent, meow!"

"I 'eard you enjoy the bloodshed, Cat God."

Was I an evil god…?

"Before we all became ghosts, this event always 'ad injuries. But no one can die now, so we're safe. I 'eard this all started when the capital was Kishiwadi under the reign of Danzir the Fifth."

"So this has a whole history, too, meow."

At last, one float remained standing, while the rest had all fallen over. The event had been quite a spectacle…

* * *

"Meow, meow, meow! That was fun, meow!"

"Then, Cat God, will you 'elp our country?"

I gave an evil little smile. This was a part of the act, too—I wasn't actually evil.

> **"No, this is not enough, meow! The world of gods runs on money, meow! I need cash, meow! Faith takes the shape of a coin, meow!"**

Now that I was properly in character, it struck me how rotten the cat god was...

"Show me your faith, meow. Otherwise, I won't give this country my protection, meow!"

I walked around atop my palanquin so that all the audience members could see how smug I was. I didn't feel embarrassed at all now—my transformation was complete.

"Very well. Then we'll show ya our faith."

As Muu spoke, she taped a coin to my leg. It was cold... I was used to the sensation of coins in my hand, after all.

"What are you doing, meow...?"

That was the line in the script, but it was also how I felt.

"I offer this coin to ya, Cat God."

Yes—apparently coins were offered to the cat god by sticking them directly to the god's body.

The ghost staff members came up to me and started sticking coins on my face and arms. This was less fun... There sure were some weird festivals out there...

Stick, stick, stick, stick, stick, stick, stick, stick...

By the time the fifth coin had been taped to my cheek, I yelled, "That's enough, meow! Enough! I promise to help grow your country!"

"Ha-ha-ha! Thanks for your blessing!" Muu kneeled before me.

I peeled off all the coins and scattered them among the people watching at the foot of the palanquin. Each coin one picked up was said to bring great profits, and I could see the ghosts crowding around.

"People always 'urt themselves pickin' up those coins," explained Muu.

This whole festival sounded like a bloodbath...

I patted Muu's head as she kneeled before me.

"My divine power is now yours, meow~ Be thankful, meow~"

The narrative was a little rough around the edges, but the festival had some semblance of a storyline. The ruler entertained the cat god, who then shared its power with the country.

"Long live the queen!" "To sound health!" "May my business prosper!"

The ghosts in the audience were all yelling. In a way, it was a touching little ending.

With my role as cat god fulfilled, I should be able to turn back to my normal self now. But then Nahna Nahna approached the palanquin where Muu and I sat.

Huh. Nahna Nahna coming over wasn't part of the script... Or maybe she was here to collect me, now that my job was over.

"Mighty Cat God, there is another sovereign who wishes for your power. This is a special case, but do you think you could oblige?"

I had a terrible feeling about this, but I knew I couldn't say no. Even the most tyrannical gods could read the room.

"Very well, meow. I'll make an exception, meow. Bring them over, meow."

Pecora immediately spread her wings and lifted into the air. There was a great look of delight on her face.

I was right! This is terrible!

"I knew it was you, Elder Sister~ ♪ Now that I'm close up, I'm absolutely sure! You're so cute!"

* * *

She'd found me out!

"I do not understand, meow... Of whom do you speak, meow?"

Nahna Nahna, behind Pecora, said with a totally flat expression, "I informed our guest of honor about your identity, since I believed it to be my responsibility as minister."

She did this on purpose!

I'd let my guard down. Making Beelzebub promise not to tell anyone wasn't enough. This was a festival for the Thursa Thursa Kingdom—I should've been thinking about keeping Nahna Nahna quiet!

Pecora kneeled before me. "O Cat God, please offer your power to the demons."

I didn't have a choice. I had to play the part.

"...Very well, meow. Be thankful, meow." I patted Pecora's head.

"Wow... Your hands are so warm, Cat God~"

Well, if this is all it takes to make her happy...

"Had enough yet, meow?"

"Could you pet me for another five minutes, please?"

Five minutes was too long, but a little more couldn't hurt.

Meanwhile, Nahna Nahna brought over a very handsomely decorated box.

"Cat God, we thank you humbly for your presence today. It's not much, but please accept this small gift."

"What is it, meow?"

We had moved beyond the script at this point, but I decided to keep putting *meow* at the end of my sentences anyway.

"Nothing less than a potpourri pouch made of the finest catnip."

Nahna Nahna slowly opened the lid of the box. It was the type with a sliding top, and inside was a small cloth pouch sitting prettily in the center.

My instincts—no, someone else's—began to scream: *I want it! I want it!*

The next moment—

—a spectral cat leaped out of my body!

The feline spirit pounced on the pouch in total bliss. I guess the stuff is irresistible even in the afterlife.

This strategy was like scattering some catnip a short distance from the radiator to lure the cat away.

"But if that's all you had to do, then you could've done it two weeks ago…"

"We only open this box during the cat god festival. It'll lose its smell if we open it too often."

It was just like how some Buddha statues were only shown to the public once a year.

"Good for you, ey?" Muu pointed to my head as she spoke. "All yer cat parts are gone. Good for you."

I put my hand to my head in relief.

That's right! Now that the spirit was out of me—

"My cat ears are gone!"

I reached around to my butt. The tail was gone, too.

"Yes! I'm back to normal!" I threw my hands in the air.

There came a quiet applause from somewhere close by. Pecora was smiling and clapping for me.

"How wonderful, Elder Sister~ ♪"

"…Yeah. A lot happened, but all's well that ends well."

"That said, I wouldn't mind you putting on cat ears every once in a while~"

"No."

"But I am not the only one hoping for it."

Pecora turned to watch as Laika approached.

Embarrassed, Laika said, "Lady Azusa, I don't think it would be a bad idea if you put on cat ears now and then… It might serve as a nice change of pace…"

"Two votes won't convince me!"

Once the festival was over, I paid a visit to the Thursa Thursa Kingdom's cat café.

I lay down, resting my head on a lion's stomach. As I lay there, other cats and tigers came to snooze with me.

"Phew. The exhaustion hits all at once when the festival ends, huh?"

One of the nearby cats meowed. I felt like it was agreeing with me.

"Cats really are the best thing for soothing one's soul~"

As I lay surrounded by soft fur and whiskers, I could feel my spirit recovering.

"Sheesh. Don't melt," Muu said, approaching.

"I just finished a big job. I'm allowed to laze around for a bit."

"Guess so. I won't fault ya. But—" Muu's eyes darted to a patch of empty air.

"—don't let another cat spirit get in ya."

There was probably a cat ghost where she was looking...

"J-just let me use the bag of catnip if that happens..."

She was right, though. Last time I was here, I'd wound up with ears and a tail. If I came here to recuperate and ended up as someone's soul radiator again, I'd be caught in an endless loop...

Just then, a few of the cats lifted their heads to watch as a customer entered the café.

Ost Ande the reaper had arrived, a number of her tendrils waving around.

"...Hello, kitties."

I quietly gave Ost Ande some space.

It was best to let sleeping cats lie...

WE THOUGHT ABOUT THIS YEAR'S **WITCH'S HOUSE CAFÉ**

That day, I went shopping in Flatta with Falfa and Shalsha. Sandra came along, too.

Sandra wasn't a very straightforward person, so whenever I asked if she'd like to join, she'd usually turn me down by saying she would prefer to photosynthesize or something.

But that didn't mean she never wanted to come along, nor was she a shut-in. Of course, since she spent most of the day outside in the vegetable garden, *shut-in* probably didn't apply, either way.

For that reason, I made sure to invite her along whenever I could. It was a bit of extra work, but I had a feeling most kids were like Sandra. I was cranky when I was a kid, too.

Falfa and Shalsha, on the other hand, were unusually obedient. But that was fine, too.

"Hmm. The townsfolk are different today," observed Sandra.

She'd noticed that something felt different about Flatta and was busily looking right and left.

"They're carrying big pieces of cloth and constructing things," she continued. "Oh, that's right—isn't it Dance Festival season soon?"

She'd arrived at the answer so quickly; I was shocked.

"That's right! You remembered, Sandra. I didn't think you were all that interested in human festivals, but you're right. They *are* getting ready for the Dance Festival!"

"Plants remember well what happens in a year. We have to make sure flowers bloom in the right season, you know."

I see. That was a good, plantlike reason. A cherry blossom tree that bloomed in autumn wouldn't have a good time at all… That would be like if someone got the date of a wedding wrong and showed up a day late.

"Mommy, are we doing the Witch's House Café this year?"

Falfa looked at me expectantly.

That's right—in the past, the family would hold a one-day-only café up in the house in the highlands the day before the Dance Festival.

Not to brag, but it always gets very busy. Actually yeah, I am bragging. That's exactly what I'm doing. That said, it's so successful that I have every reason to be proud.

In fact, I got the feeling Falfa was asking about it now precisely because she knew it had done so well.

"Shalsha believes we can make it even more exciting than last year," Shalsha said frankly, her enthusiasm obvious.

I, however, couldn't agree so easily. But I couldn't stay silent, either, so I said in a low voice:

"Hmm… You're right, I guess we'll have to start thinking about the Witch's House Café…"

I must have sounded half-hearted to the others.

Falfa and Shalsha looked up at me with surprise, so I added, "This is a very important matter, so we'll have a good talk about it tonight after dinner."

That night, after Halkara came home, we had our evening meal.

Afterward, everyone stayed in their seats.

*Incidentally, the conversation wouldn't go anywhere if Halkara was smashed, so I limited her to two drinks.

"All right. Now, we're going to hold a little meeting so we can decide what to do about this year's Witch's House Café!"

"Falfa wants it to be big! I think Miss Beelzebub and the others will help, too!" Falfa said as her hand shot up in the air.

I was very happy she felt that way. And I agreed that Beelzebub would indeed help us every year, even if we didn't invite her.

"Madam Teacher, we have some space in front of the Halkara Pharmaceuticals Museum. You can leave matters in Nascúte to me."

Halkara was keen on making some money, it seemed.

"I can ask Muu, too. Maybe the Thursa Thursa Kingdom can lend us a hand! They might even volunteer!"

I was delighted to hear Rosalie's suggestion. I could tell how enthusiastic everyone was.

But that was why this was so painful for me!

"That's precisely the problem!" I said, getting to my feet. "Our Witch's House Café was a huge success last year. But it's all gotten *way* too big. Vania even brought over tables and chairs in her leviathan form. It's become so massive that it's ceased to be a café..."

In terms of size, it was more like a huge beer garden. The demons Beelzebub brought along had done construction, too. To be honest, I didn't even remember how many people were working on the day.

"So, uh... What I was originally going for was a little out-of-the-way café where people could catch their breath for a moment. But now, it's grown into a huge annual event..."

That's what troubled me.

"At this rate, it will only get bigger... And soon, it'll be known not only throughout Nanterre but the entire country... It'll completely eclipse Flatta's Dance Festival, the original main event..."

The scope was expanding beyond my control. In fact, it had already reached that point the year before.

"Indeed—if tens of thousands of people were to swarm the area, it may attract those wanting to establish commercial stalls, thieves targeting festivalgoers, and other similar problems…," Laika mused, tilting her head in thought. "That would not be good for Flatta."

A café that had tens of thousands of customers in one day wasn't really much of a café anymore.

"Exactly. If this keeps getting bigger and bigger, we might end up spending most of the year preparing… And then we'd just be an events company."

There were a huge number of events in this world, for some reason, and I was sure none of them started preparation only a month beforehand. They had to recruit vendors, rent out event spaces, look for staff—with all that stuff to think about, they would *have* to start at least a year in advance.

Even when it came to school cultural festivals, no class chose what they were going to do with only one week to spare. If they were dealing with food, they'd have to send out special notifications, too. The cultural festival committees had to start work well ahead of the event.

The Witch's House Café wasn't just starting out—we were waist-deep in the swamp of big event-dom.

"It would probably be difficult to downsize at this point, though, right?" I said. "Word is already spreading, and we know we'll get even more attendees this time around."

"Madam Teacher? You're calling the customers 'attendees.' You must already be thinking of it as a big event subconsciously…"

"Oh gosh. You're right, Halkara."

Cafés didn't usually call their customers "attendees."

To be honest, as the Dance Festival drew closer, I had been starting to worry about how we were going to get through this.

Tears of joy are a normal reaction to a successful business, but right now I just wanted to cry for real.

"Then we should just cancel, Mistress," Flatorte said breezily. "It's not like we've told anyone we're doing it this year. No one has any right to complain if we don't."

"You truly never think about what you are saying, do you? The café is big enough that it affects the attendance numbers of the entire Dance Festival. We cannot simply cancel it...," Laika said with a sigh.

"Why do we have to worry about Flatta? That has nothing to do with us. Would fewer people cause the whole festival to fail? Don't they do it every year regardless?"

"Mgh... If we could push through with logic alone, Lady Azusa would not be so troubled... Think about it for moment, won't you...?"

Mindful people like Laika always had it rough in situations like this... That said, I did understand what Flatorte was trying to say. Laika was right—it was very logical.

It wasn't like the village itself was asking us to do this. We didn't *have* to. But if we decided not to do it, that might still cause a commotion in the village.

I glanced at Halkara. Maybe this was a good time to ask someone with a managerial perspective.

"Oh, then why don't we go with a numbered ticket system?" she said.

"A numbered ticket system?"

That was unexpected.

"Yes, yes! We could issue numbered tickets for the café, and only the ones with tickets could come in. That way, the café will never be overcrowded."

"Shalsha thinks that if you weren't always inebriated, you'd regularly save the day, Miss Halkara."

"Is that spite I sense, Shalsha...? Am I really that bad when I'm drunk...?"

"The fact that you aren't aware of it, Miss Halkara, is already a sign you need to think about your alcohol consumption. Many times, you have nearly reached a point of no return."

Falfa's expression was genuinely worried.

Halkara winced sheepishly. "I'll be as careful as I can from now on… Um, back to the numbered ticket idea."

That's right—we weren't talking about how to fix Halkara's drinking habit.

"And we can write on the ticket, *Your ticket is only valid for the whatever-o'clock time slot. Please come a little earlier. If you are not here on time, we may allow another guest to enter ahead of you.* That should help us control the crowd. What do you think?"

"Hmm, hmm. Even if we can whittle down the attendance numbers, if more people than capacity show up, it would still cause problems. In that case, maybe this is our only choice."

Since the café wasn't a public service, it would probably be fine to limit attendance.

"That will allow us to keep running the café, so I think we should try it."

"Oh, but there's a chance it might not turn out so well…" Halkara went slightly pale. She must have discovered a downside. "If we were to implement a numbered ticket system for something so popular, scalpers would line up to buy the tickets. Then they'd resell them at an inflated price, which would be very bad…"

Crap! I hadn't even considered a ticket resale problem!

"And if the tickets go for too high a price and no one buys them, we might hand out all the tickets and get no customers. That'd be a tragedy… Still, we can't charge money for the tickets. Maybe it would be feasible if we only served one set meal, but that's not how people order at cafés. No one will want to decide what they want weeks in advance… Oh, this isn't going to work! It just isn't! I take it all back!"

"I have no idea what just happened, but it looks like the one who came up with the idea is voluntarily withdrawing it."

I never dreamed I'd ever be worrying about ticket resale issues in this world…

But considering how popular the café was, I was sure there would be people with no interest in the event itself who would try to get a ticket just to sell it for a profit.

"Being alive is rough. It's always money, money, money, isn't it?" Rosalie remarked thoughtfully.

"The balance of supply and demand is so difficult… Running a shop is really hard!"

Then Shalsha slowly raised her hand.

"Do you have an idea, Shalsha?"

"Shalsha thinks that one of the reasons the café is so popular is that it only happens once a year. Therefore, many people come because they know they only have one day to visit."

"Well. I suppose that's correct."

"Then the best solution is to make it no longer special. If we run the café all the time, we can avoid most of these problems. That is why I think we should open a permanent Witch's House Café around Flatta or Nascúte!"

As Shalsha spoke, her eyes grew wider and wider. She seemed very enthusiastic about this idea.

"This keeps getting more and more complicated!"

I had never once thought about opening an actual café.

I didn't want to shut down my child's idea, but…I didn't think that was the solution, either.

"That'd mean working at a restaurant… And I feel like that's the opposite of relaxing…"

Every morning, we'd have to do prep, and after we closed every evening, we'd have to clean up…

Oh no, I could already see how much trouble it would be. At that point, my job wouldn't be witch—it'd be restaurateur!

"Why don't we just open it whenever we feel like it?" said Flatorte. "Whoever happened on us at the right time could consider themselves lucky, and it'd be a lot easier on us."

Laika gave her another exasperated look.

"Then there is no point in a permanent establishment, is there? And if it is only open for a few days, we will have the problem of swarming customers again."

"Shalsha thinks there is no reason for members of the family to always be working there. Anyone should be able to cook the food so long as we teach them. None of us cooks as their main job, but we've managed thus far. We'll be fine."

So Shalsha was of the opinion that we should only be involved in operations…

I put my head down on the table.

"That might solve our congestion problem, but…at that point, it's not an out-of-the-way café anymore."

My original goal was long gone.

"It was not that kind of café last year, either, Mom."

"Shalsha's correct. Madam Teacher, once popularity hits fever pitch, we can't hide anymore. Every gourmet knows all the best hidden restaurants in the capital."

Shalsha and Halkara delivered the coup de grâce. I guess this was what it meant to be popular.

"You're right. If anyone wants to run the café, they're more than welcome to. I'm stepping down…"

After I accidentally reached max level, I'd had my relaxed life interrupted on more than a few occasions, but this café's popularity seemed set to destroy it entirely.

I needed to remember my original intent and stop pushing myself. I didn't have to do it if I didn't want to.

Just then, the door flung open.

What was going on? Was that Sandra coming in?

No, Sandra was in her chair. She'd just fallen asleep, since she wasn't interested in the topic.

Then who was at the door?

"I overheard everything, man!"

Misjantie the pine spirit had come into the house.

"…How were you even listening?" I asked.

"Oh, I wasn't eavesdropping, man! You've got a pine tree growing nearby, yeah? The pine tree just passed it along."

"Maybe I should cut it down."

She *was* eavesdropping. I hated the thought of other people listening in.

"Don't do that, man! Without that pine tree, I'll have no reason to keep the Flatta branch around!"

She'd made us plant that tree as a part of her strategy, hadn't she...?

"What would you like to do about this, then, Miss Misjantie?"

Laika stood and made her way toward the kitchen. I bet she was going to make some tea for Misjantie. She was so good.

"I want you to let me run the Witch's House Café, man."

I didn't think we'd find someone willing to run it so quickly!

"I gotta keep things diversified, otherwise I won't be able to keep operating my pine shrines. I'm just trying to do everything I can, man."

"Hmm... So long as you don't underpay or overwork the locals, I'd be happy to let you do it. Oh, and don't get greedy and try to mark up the salads by claiming the vegetables all came from the Witch of the Highlands's garden or something."

"You don't trust me at all, Azusa... I'm shocked, man..."

Sorry, but you reap what you sow. Misjantie and Fighsly were evenly matched when it came to greed. If anything, Fighsly was the one with a sound grasp of economics; Misjantie was way more of a problem.

"Don't worry about that, man. I'm planning on calling on the temple workers to do the job. I've gotta go say hi to some of the staff, so I don't really have a choice."

"Doesn't that mean you'd be making the priests take food service jobs...? Isn't it kind of a big deal to make people do work they're not suited for...?"

Misjantie shook her head, then let her body droop.

"A lot of the priests have fallen on hard times because they don't make enough, man... No priest can put food on the table with faith alone nowadays. It'd be perfect if I could just create employment for them, y'know... I've got enough to staff the place, so they wouldn't be working overtime..."

This sounded way too real.

"Fine... Then I'll let you take care of the Witch's House Café, Misjantie..."

After she admitted she needed employment for her priests, it became very hard to turn her down. Even if there were problems, this was still a café we were talking about. I doubted anyone would be injured or miserable working there.

"Thanks so much, man! I know this is a well-known establishment, so I'm gonna give it my all!"

"It's only ever been open for a total of two days, so I don't know if you can really call it a 'well-known establishment'..."

It seemed rude to equate it to restaurants that had earned their reputation over years of service.

"At any rate, we'll teach you the recipes. Everything else we'll leave up to you."

"Got it, man. I'll give you a shout once the shop's set up and the priests arrive. I'll only open it once the priests have gone through training and can re-create the flavors flawlessly."

"Please stop talking about it like it's a famous restaurant with a long and distinguished history."

I personally thought the food was pretty good, but the café became popular because of its novelty, not what it served.

Still, if this allowed us to start business well before the Dance Festival, we could almost certainly ease congestion. Travelers could come during the festival, and those who lived nearby could come another day. I bet very few would want to spend a week traveling just to come to the café.

At that point, I was thinking we'd basically solved the café problem, but...I was naive.

"Hey, Big Sis, can I have a sec?" Rosalie said to me from overhead. "I think the biggest draw of the Witch's House Café was actually a certain someone's presence..."

When she finished, she turned to look at Laika.

"...*Gasp!* Miss Rosalie, please do not insinuate such things! I have done nothing particularly impressive or fantastic...," Laika protested, her face going red.

But the way she protested was so cute that it kind of invalidated her point. Rosalie was right. Laika in her maid uniform was practically legendary. That might sound like an exaggeration, but it was surprisingly close to the truth.

"If she's not there the day before the Dance Festival, I'm pretty sure people will be disappointed... I can't force her to do it, but..."

"Y-you misunderstand! A café is not a place where people go to see a particular staff member! It is a haven of r-relaxation!"

What Laika was saying was true, but I knew a lot of our visitors last year had come just to see her.

"Laika, please! You've gotta help out, even if it's just for a short period of time, man! Just a little while! The time right after opening is critical for places like this, man!" Misjantie begged. It all felt a bit dramatic, but Misjantie's entire temple system always seemed on the verge of bankruptcy, so she probably had no choice but to go all out.

Laika seemed defeated, too.

"Okay, but only because it is a special occasion... I have no intention of dealing with customers for days in a row, all right?" Laika was setting forth some conditions for her agreement.

"That's perfect, man. We want it to feel really special, so once a year's all we need."

Incidentally, Misjantie was a spirit people actually worshipped, so I sometimes wished she'd speak with a little more dignity. But that was neither here nor there.

It looked like the problems surrounding the Witch's House Café were going to be solved. I felt like a weight had been lifted from my shoulders.

◇

The café was built in an empty spot about halfway between the towns of Flatta and Nascúte. Construction moved quickly, probably because a tree spirit was in charge, and it was completed two days after they received permission to start building.

"Oh, you're making its official name House of the Pine Spirit," I said. "That works for me."

Since I wasn't going to be there, this name would be much more accurate than the Witch's House Café.

"Yes. I didn't want people complaining about Laika's absence, so I decided to go with this name instead."

It sounded petty, but I had the feeling it was a very shrewd decision.

"Okay, man. I'm gonna ask you to check how the food tastes once the priests arrive. They should be getting their oracles from the pines right about now, so they'll be here soon."

I wondered how it would feel to be a priest receiving an oracle from the spirit they worshipped asking them to work at a restaurant... But maybe that devotion meant even bizarre oracles wouldn't faze them.

"To be honest, I wanna give the priests better salaries... I told 'em when I hired 'em that this was a declining temple, though. They were given fair warning, but... Man."

"That sure is tough..."

Unfortunately, some religions were growing, and some were dying out. That's just what things were like out there in the world.

That aside, there'd been something bothering me since the moment I got here.

"Why'd you pick such an awkward place to build the café? It's not close to either town."

It wasn't in Nascúte, and it wasn't in Flatta, either. Maybe it was perfect for those who went back and forth between the two, but it was weirdly inconvenient for most.

"The biggest reason was 'cause the land was cheap, man."

"That's not a reason I was expecting to hear from a spirit…"

Well, I guess if she wasn't strapped for cash, she wouldn't have offered to run the place.

"And out here, man, we're not gonna be bothering any neighbors even with a big crowd. If we put it in Flatta, it'd get crowded and awkward during the festival. I don't wanna deal with any complaints."

"There's nothing pine spirity about any of this…"

She was cautious, though. I'd give her that.

"Also, this is the place where the pines grow the healthiest."

The spot was, in fact, off the main road and through what was basically a pine tree tunnel. Maybe it was due to associations from my previous life, but the pines made the place seem very Japanese. It almost felt like the garden of some fancy Japanese-style restaurant.

"You're sincere in the weirdest ways, Misjantie, considering you saved that reason for last."

If she was trying to act the part, that would have been the first thing she said.

"Feelings are important, but so is money, man. And the reality is, money usually wins out."

"Please don't say that in front of your priests…"

They'd probably be shocked.

"Oh yeah, there's a little temple for worship in the back."

Just as she said, in the back of the building was a small stone shrine with the words *Pine Spirit Misjantie* carved into it. The building resembled a house with a little shrine in the yard.

In front of the shrine was a notice board.

"You really need to stop begging for offerings whenever you get the chance!"

"Actually, seizing every opportunity is the key to success! Every coin counts, man! If someone give a single gold with feeling, you gotta accept it!"

I couldn't believe she was trying to turn begging into some kind of lecture on ethics.

"But you'd be happier getting a hundred or a thousand gold over just one, right?"

"Of course, man!"

The more I learned about spirits and gods, the less faith I had in them. It felt a lot like snagging a dream job, only to be hit by the harsh realities of the industry...

Just as Misjantie said, temple priests arrived from all over a few days later, so I headed back out to the House of the Pine Spirit to help teach them our recipes.

When I got there, this is what the priests told me:

"I am so thankful for this opportunity. We were only just scraping by after turning more than half of our lot into carriage parking." "We sold our land to a company that built a three-story shop on the property, and we've been practicing in a small corner in the back." "The pine on our lot has withered and looks terrible, but we have no money to replant it." "One cannot make a living on faith alone these days, you know? A second or third job is a must."

All of them were in deep financial trouble!

Misjantie clapped her hands and addressed the priests.

"Okay, everyone, enough misery poker. We're gonna have you all perfectly replicate the food from the Witch's House Café, man!"

"Very well, great Pine Spirit Misjantie." "I will never forget how you appeared to us in this manner." "I do not regret my faith!" "We will make this business thrive!"

I was impressed they could stay faithful in the face of such a casual spirit!

"You all listening? Now, Azusa is gonna teach you how to cook everything on the menu. Treat her like another pine spirit, man."

"Understood!" "I will lick your boots if you ask me to!" "I will not complain even if you poke me with a pine needle." "If you wish, you may hit me with a pinecone at the speed of a professionally pitched baseball."

They were humbling themselves in the weirdest ways, and I hated it!

"Just curious," I said, "but have all of you met the pine spirit in the flesh before? Aren't you shocked or anything?"

"She is just as casual as the oracle foretold." "Based on the description I got, I would feel more betrayed if I were met with an old man with a graying beard." "A follower goes down with their spirit." "She's even cuter than my wife."

I felt like I was at a village meeting.

Though I worried about their futures, I was lucky that the priests were so earnest and hardworking. They picked up the task at hand pretty quickly, too. It wasn't like we had some super-secret forbidden sauce or anything, so all the food was easy to re-create.

"All right. I'd say they've got the flavors down pretty well now," I said as Misjantie and I sampled the dishes.

The priests were on their break and had gone into to town to enjoy themselves.

"Good, man. Well, so long as we get decent business from Flatta or Nascúte and I can put away a little bit of cash, I'll call it a success."

"You don't have a lot of passion for this, do you, Misjantie? I know you need money, but you don't seem very motivated to strike it rich."

That's what made her different from Fighsly. The latter would do anything to turn a profit.

Misjantie flashed me a cynical smile. "Well, compared to the real Witch's House Café, we don't have much of a draw. This place is run by middle-aged guys who can barely keep their own temples going... It's not gonna be as successful as a place run entirely by cute girls. You gotta understand how important the cute factor is, man..."

I wasn't sure how to react to that.

"I mean... It's not like we were running a café staffed by popular actresses from the royal capital or something. We aren't that special..."

"Azusa, dude, that's not it. It's the visual. We just can't compare. We're not gonna strike it big even if we replicate the food perfectly. The food's important, too, but it's just one of many elements, man."

"Please don't say that about running a *restaurant*."

I had really complicated feelings about what she was saying, b-but anyway! Hopefully, the House of the Pine Spirit would find its way to success.

The House of the Pine Spirit opened about one month before the Dance Festival.

According to Misjantie, things were going steadily, and they'd started off on a better foot than she'd expected.

It might sound weird to be pleased about a business only doing so-so, but personally, I was relieved. It seemed like this would be a good point of compromise to solve the café's congestion problem. I felt my stress finally melting away. I could participate in the Dance Festival, free from worry.

That was how I'd originally wanted to spend the Dance Festival, so you might say I was starting over.

But, again, I was naive.

* * *

One nice day as the festival was approaching, someone paid us a visit early in the morning. It was Natalie, from the guild.

"Great Witch of the Highlands, we ask that you please hold the Witch's House Café again this year!"

"Oh, uh. Well, there's a place called the House of the Pine Spirit that's—"

"We know your location has moved!"

I didn't think what we'd done counted as moving locations, but I knew what Natalie was trying to say.

"But it must be a café with you and your family as staff! Please! *Please!* We would love it if you would go all out for the festival! That is the villagers' consensus! If only for the duration of the festival, do you think you and your family could appear at the new location?"

Ugh… It was hard to turn down a request from the town itself…

Laika arrived with a cup of tea for Natalie.

"Um… Though it wasn't my preference, I will be working at the café the day before the festival…"

"Yes! I have heard already, Miss Laika! We expect great things from you!"

"Who told you…? Oh, I suppose it was someone from the café…"

That seemed likely… Misjantie wasn't going to bury information that might attract customers.

"Still! It's all of you who make it the Witch's House Café! If only Laika is there, then it would be the Laika Is Cute House!"

"And I would not work anywhere with a name like that," she said flatly.

Same here. I'd hate to work at a place called the Witch Is Cute House, too.

"And so there is good reason for all of you to get together and put on the Witch's House Café! It is the biggest event of the Dance Festival! Everyone in the village agrees!"

"We've only held it for two years, you know. Are you really okay with that?"

"Yes! You have lived much longer than the festival has existed anyway!"

Natalie had hit me where it hurt. She was right... From my perspective, the festival was still pretty new.

And not to repeat myself, but it was very difficult to turn down a request from the village. They were always looking out for me, so it felt wrong to refuse them...

"Um, even though the café is in between Flatta and Nascúte, there's a chance it's going to be a lot more crowded than it was last year. No, I'm *sure* it will be."

"The guild is currently gathering adventurers to work as traffic control. We will do everything in our power to make this work! And we're establishing a numbered ticket system so that not too many people come!"

"But what about scalpers—?"

"We've hired guards and adventurers to combat them!"

They'd thought more carefully about this than I expected! After all that, I really couldn't say no.

"Fine... But we'll only do it for one day, on the eve of the festival..."

At the very least, *I* would. I didn't think it was right to ask Laika to do this alone.

"Thank you so much! That's my main task for today all done!"

Natalie went home in high spirits.

Afterward, Misjantie paid us a visit.

"Hey, uh, if possible, could all of you come work at the café the day before the festival? And not just—"

"I know," I said. "We'll be there."

"Please, man, just— Oh. You'll do it?"

There was no other choice—we'd simply have to give it our all!

WE OPENED THE WITCH'S HOUSE CAFÉ AGAIN

And so in the end, we held the Witch's House Café again that year.

We weren't using the house in the highlands, however, but Misjantie's café. It was already in operation and had all the fixtures we needed, so we didn't have to do too much in terms of preparation.

And we had the maid uniforms from last year.

"I just tried on mine. I haven't worn it since last year, but the moths didn't get it or anything. I think it'll do its job on the day."

"Madam Teacher, for some reason, it's much too tight around my chest, and I can't close the buttons..."

"Are you bragging?!"

Halkara seemed to be attempting that kind of humblebrag where you pretended to be having trouble for some enviable reason, and it was *not* a good look. Not a good look at all.

"No I'm not... I haven't eaten all that much meat, but have I gotten fat?"

"You might not eat meat, but you drink like a fish."

"Oh, I suppose it all went to my chest, then."

"You are bragging!"

Normally, someone's chest wasn't the only thing that got bigger.

"If it's really that tight, Halkara, then just rip it a little."

Flatorte was giving awful advice. Irreversible solutions were not recommended for things like this. And besides, walking around with a shirt ripped at the chest would be even more disgraceful.

I was finished getting dressed, so I helped Sandra put her outfit on next.

"Oh... This is so uncomfortable... I wish to hide in the earth..."

"Don't hide with these clothes on, okay? You just need to drop by on the day. We're more like set dressing this time, after all."

I had a feeling that Sandra was starting to show more interest in her appearance now, but the maid outfit had nothing to do with fashion. It was technically just a work uniform, so she must not see any reason to put up with the discomfort.

"Okay. I'll take little breaks now and then to photosynthesize."

Her comment made her sound like a smoker, but plants probably weren't suited to indoor work.

"And the pines in this area are very well-behaved."

"...Right. Well, I don't know anything about that, so just be sure to get along with the other plants, okay?"

Next, Rosalie popped out from the floor. She was already wearing her uniform thanks to my changing spell.

"You're a lot more businesslike this year, Big Sis."

"If anything, we were trying way too hard during the last two festivals. I think our concept this time should be 'natural.'"

We weren't going to push ourselves or try too hard. We'd take care of things as they arose. No one person could be doing their best all the time anyway. If this was going to require constant effort, then it would've failed at the planning stage.

I wasn't trying to open a dozen more branches this year or anything like that, so there was no need to overthink it. We'd just take it easy and run the café.

"...But that's just a goal," I concluded.

"Your smile isn't reaching your eyes, Big Sis…"

"Even if *we* manage to stay natural, our friends and acquaintances might show up and cause problems… And there's not much we can do about that. We'll just have to deal with whatever happens."

The demons dropping by wouldn't be too big a deal. It was the gods I was worried about. Thankfully, I didn't think anyone held any grudges against me…

"Oh, when Beelzebub stops by, I'll have to remind her not to come on a leviathan."

The people around Flatta had gotten used to it, but it might give out-of-towners a heart attack. And if she had leviathans hauling cargo, we'd be right back to the previous year's scale.

Beelzebub, incidentally, did come by two days later.

"Of course. I plan on using a wyvern this year. 'Tis fine."

"Good. A wyvern should be all right."

I had a feeling my idea of what was acceptable had shifted dramatically over the years.

"Oh, and, Azusa. Are you fine without me working this year?"

Beelzebub was a minister, and here she was, asking me if I needed help like we were students preparing for a school festival.

"I appreciate the offer, but we're staying modest this year, so don't worry about it. The café's location makes it seem like a little hideaway, too."

"I see, I see. 'Twas originally a small festival for a small village, no? I suppose that is most suitable."

Exactly. The Dance Festival wasn't that big, and it wasn't originally a big draw for tourists. The villagers hadn't even considered the possibility until two years ago.

But though the event was small, that didn't mean the happiness it brought was insignificant. It was the perfect size for a village like Flatta. I was glad to hear that Beelzebub understood.

"Then we shall do as we please."

"Yeah, sure. —Wait. What do you mean, 'as you please'...? What are you going to do...?"

But Beelzebub had gone to Falfa and Shalsha's room, so I couldn't ask her anything else.

"It'll be fine. Probably. I hope..."

At last, the eve of the Dance Festival arrived.

Typically, a phrase like *at last* would be used for the Dance Festival itself, but we were running the café the day before, so that was the date we'd been awaiting.

The family and I all visited a few places in Flatta on our way to the café.

Nothing was out of the ordinary so far. The village felt like it always did during the Dance Festival.

Next to the guild was a temporary booth with a sign that said WITCH'S HOUSE CAFÉ TICKETS HERE, and there was a line trailing away from it, but...I decided to consider that a minor variation.

In addition, there was another line where the food stalls always were. That was different, too...

"Another weird stall, I see."

There was a familiar-looking dark elf selling pots and platters.

It was the Phantom Thief Canhein. She had infiltrated Halkara Pharmaceuticals Museum to steal an artifact once before. Though perhaps *steal* was the wrong word...

"Ah-ha-ha! I am Canhein, the Phantom Thief! I obtain my items cheaply, and I sell them at a competitive price! I am engaging in trade that allows me to face both the sun and the elven forests!"

"In that case, you don't need to call yourself a thief anymore," I said.

"Oh, hey there! What do you think? Interested in buying anything? This platter here was the work of a once-great potter…or so it appears, but it's only a very accurate fake, so I'm selling it for almost nothing!"

"You're still so honest. I don't want to carry it around, so I'll drop by on my way back."

From there, we traveled along the main road.

The House of the Pine Spirit (which was the Witch's House Café for the day) was just a little farther. The road was just a normal countryside path, but we took our time traveling.

"Lady Azusa, there are no lines. Perhaps the numbered ticket system is working."

Laika was right; I didn't see any ridiculous lines along the side of the road.

"We've only just left the village. If people were lined up all the way out here, it'd be bad news for us. There aren't any other shops between here and the—"

"Lady Azusa, it seems there are some stalls ahead of us…"

What? Not a lot of people went this way; setting up a stall here wouldn't bring in any profits. If human vendors had shown up due to the crowds the previous year, I'd feel a little guilty.

But in fact, there weren't any human shopkeepers at all. The rows and rows of stalls were all being run by demons!

"I had a feeling they might be up to something, but I never imagined they'd pull something like this!"

As I spoke, Beelzebub flew over to us from some distance away.

"We're not making any trouble," she said. "We have permission to set up shop here."

There was a bundle of permits in Beelzebub's hands. I saw the Flatta mayor's signature, so it appeared they were obeying the rules.

"Okay. Do what you like. But you know Flatta's jurisdiction ends along this road, right?"

"We have permission from the province and the city at the other end of the road, too."

"Well, all right. If it's all legal, then I have nothing more to say."

As we walked along, I spotted Pondeli's and Nosonia's stalls. They were selling games and clothes, respectively. They were actually doing business related to their real jobs.

"It's so good to see you, Miss Azusa! You saved my life, so I'll offer you something on the house!"

"Thanks, Nosonia. But I'd have to carry anything you gave me for the rest of the day, so I'll come back later."

Nosonia was apparently selling clothes with minor faults in them at a lower price, like an outlet store. But games and clothes made up only a small portion of the stalls. Most of them were selling food.

"Lady Azusa, most of these places are selling very spicy food. I can see five of them in a row over there," Laika said, a bright red lamb skewer in her hands.

"Demons like spicy food."

I wanted us to simply go with the flow this year, but somehow the festival kept getting bigger.

Rosalie was looking around, too, but not at the stalls.

"Big Sis, there are so many ghosts here! It's a whole crowd!"

"Eep! That's not something I really wanted to hear…"

I suppose people did say the dead came out to play during festivals… But the ghosts weren't the most exciting thing here. The elder god Dekyari'tosde (nickname: Dekie) was walking around like it was no big deal.

What a diverse range of attendees!

Dekie looked like a normal woman with light green hair, but she could cause real danger if not treated respectfully. Actual, world-ending danger…

"OH! Look at THIS candy! It's so SPICY!"

But she seemed pleased with the festival, so we were probably safe for now... When Dekie noticed us, she waved. It didn't seem like there were any problems yet.

The stalls went on and on, even continuing past the café. It seemed they stretched all the way to Nascúte. I wondered how many there were in all.

Obviously, not all the stalls were being run by demons, but they had the clear majority.

It was impossible at this point to move around unseen...

When we entered the changing room at the back of the café, Misjantie was waiting for us.

"Thank you so much for your help today, man! Today's the only day we get to see your skills with our own eyes!"

"I mean, my skills only really amount to three days of part-time work. This is my third."

But I guess that didn't hold much weight coming from me.

Laika quickly changed into her maid outfit.

"I am never comfortable in this outfit, no matter how much I wear it... Even now, it feels as though I'm being forced to wear my academy uniform..."

"Goodness... You're like a brilliant star, Laika... So dazzling that I can barely see..."

"Please, Lady Azusa, do not exaggerate so! Th-that's not true at all!"

I was shielding my eyes for dramatic effect, but it was completely true that she looked beautiful in her uniform. The rest of the family was more or less starstruck.

"Miss Laika is so graceful and ladylike. Having her handle the customers is a real winning move, man. If only I could use her as a poster girl for my wedding campaigns."

"I totally get it. I'd love to put her in a wedding dress. But I doubt she'd agree to it..."

"I am not getting married, so I have no reason to wear one! That is where I draw the line!"

Of course, we would lose that natural effect if she was too embarrassed, so I'd just have to settle for the maid uniform.

"I knew it. Food isn't about heart. It isn't even about flavor. It's about how cute you are with the customers, man."

"That has nothing to do with food. And it's something the House of the Pine Spirit doesn't even have…"

Before opening, we all gathered together.

"Okay. The crowd is being controlled by a numbered ticket system today, so I don't think it'll be super congested like last time. If we keep our feet planted on the ground and do our jobs, it should turn out all right."

I wasn't a manager or anything, but I took on roles like this sometimes as the family's representative. I was gradually getting used to it.

"Since this is a different building than we've used in the past, it might be a little awkward at first. But don't panic. Just take it all in stride, okay?"

Afterward, I heard the family say, "Okay," and, "Understood." Their voices were all out of sync, but in a way, that was very us.

Either way, everyone looked ready to start. We were going to be okay.

It was finally time to begin.
I slowly opened the door.

"At long last, the Witch's House Café is finally op— gwegh."

I made a weird noise.

"Elder Sister! We've been so excited!"

"I shall have my fill of your customer service."

There stood Pecora, Beelzebub, Vania, and Fatla.

"We received the first numbered tickets as collateral for helping to expand the festival," Fatla said casually.

"That doesn't seem fair," I replied.

But I supposed this was how things always went. No matter how much I strove to keep things normal, those around me were always doing their best to prevent that from happening.

"How much do I have to pay to get you to write 'I love Pecora' in sauce on my food?"

"I'm sorry, ma'am, this is not that sort of establishment."

I still wanted to maintain the vibe of an out-of-the-way café if I could help it. The location was pretty close to that ideal, so I didn't want to deviate too far.

"Miss Azusa, we haven't made any prior reservations, but do you have any lunch courses?"

"This is not some famous, high-class restaurant, Vania!"

This bunch was nothing but trouble, so I brought them straight to their seats.

Okay. Time to switch gears and welcome the second group of customers.

I opened the door again.

"Sorry to keep you waiting! Welcome to the Witch's House—oof."

"Oi, Azusa! Stinkin' rich yet? Wait, ya just opened! Guess ya wouldn't know, ey?"

"Your Majesty, this is not a comedy club."

Now I stood face-to-face with Muu and Nahna Nahna.

"We got the second set of numbered tickets from the demons."

"I've been duped!"

"Right, time for a cuppa."

"You could stand to speak more politely, Your Majesty."

I could feel my energy draining as I brought them to an open seat.

"Are you all right, Madam Teacher? Would you like to swap places and spend some time in the kitchen?"

This café was the type that allowed people in the kitchen to see the whole restaurant. And it sounded like Halkara knew exactly what was going on.

"I guess so... This isn't good for my heart, so let's swap for a bit."

It wasn't like the café was going to be filled solely with people we knew all day; this wave was sure to end at some point.

I'd heard that it was annoying when friends came by your place of work just to give you a hard time, and now I knew just how true that was.

But as it turned out, I'd had it relatively easy.

When I stepped into the kitchen, I heard Halkara, who had taken my place as host, scream.

"Wh-why is my whole family here?!"

The clan had come to visit!

"We got a numbered ticket from the demons. It'd be a huge waste not to use it!" Halkara's mom replied like it was obvious.

Pecora sure was abusing the numbered ticket system! There was always room for some scheme or another. You had to look into all the risks before adopting any system, or you'd end up in a bad situation...

Having friends come by to tease you was bad, but Halkara was in an even worse position: Her *family* was here to tease her. If she'd been a teenager, she probably would have genuinely hated them for it...

"Do you have bottomless drinks?"

"No! That wouldn't make us any money! And I don't want you vomiting on the tables, so you're not allowed any alcohol!"

It seemed she had no problem being objective about her family...

"Sis, could you give us a family discount?" asked Halkara's little sister. She seemed a lot more stylish and trendy than Halkara.

"No, of course not! No funny business—you *have* to pay your bill! In fact, why don't you just give me the money now and go home?!"

I watched as the whole of Halkara's family entered the café. They looked like any old elf family at a glance, but it seemed all of them were even more careless than she was, and I could see they were going to be tough customers.

Halkara, now slumped over, went to open the door again. She was still recovering from the psychic damage of confronting her family.

B-but...Halkara! There isn't any more of your family to come visit, so all the shocks for today should be over. You just have to rally yourself, and—

Halkara screamed again.

"Wah! A bear! Bears don't even live in this area!"

Why weren't we getting any normal customers?!

"How rude. Grand Duke Polar Bear will not attack you."

Oh, I knew this voice. That was Wynona and her pet.

"You came with your bear?!" I yelled from the kitchen.

"Oh, be quiet, Stepmother. Grand Duke Polar Bear can walk on two legs, you know. It's fine. One hot tea for me and a cold glass of water for the grand duke, please."

I'm not your mother-in-law...

When, sometime later, Momma Yufufu, Curalina the jellyfish spirit, and Canimeow the moon spirit came in, I was relieved.

There was nothing normal about three spirits walking into a café, but at least they looked more like regular customers than a bear.

"Gosh, I see you have your hands full, Azusa. If you need to rest, I can take over for you, okay?"

"You *really* don't need to be that considerate."

At this point, most of my nerves were gone.

Right around that point, the wave of familiar faces stopped.

To be honest, a lot more of our acquaintances had shown up than I'd predicted.

"Madam Teacher, would you mind if we swapped again? My family keeps glancing at me, and it's irritating...," Halkara said, pointing at them. I knew how she felt, but they were still customers, and I'd prefer that she stop pointing.

"Fine. I'll cover the tables..."

* * *

After that, it was all normal customers, and I finally got into the swing of things.

Just as I'd thought, our modus operandi this year was much closer to my original vision of the café. Thanks to the numbered ticket system, we didn't have anyone lining up early in the morning. I knew it was useless to dwell on the past, but the number of customers we'd had last year and the year before was simply not normal.

This year, however, certain customers seemed determined to poke fun at us…

"Excuse me, waiter, I'd like the usual, please."

"You don't have a usual. Stop acting like a regular."

Listen to Beelzebub, talking nonsense. She was definitely teasing me.

"And make sure 'tis the girls who bring me my food. It will taste better that way."

"I'm sorry, ma'am, but we don't offer that sort of service—"

"Please!"

Beelzebub looked so serious that it almost scared me.

"Fine. I'll allow it…"

Afterward, Falfa and Shalsha entered the room. They looked like they hadn't brought anything with them, but a cart carrying the food (a trolley?) followed behind them, pushed by Sandra. I bet this was Sandra's idea.

"Here comes the cart! Please make room~!"

"The plates and food are hot. Make sure not to spill anything when you take them."

When the food arrived, Beelzebub began to get excited.

"They all look so good! You're both such good cooks!"

"Miss Halkara was the one who made it~"

"Oh, those are just minor details. This is *your* food, since you brought it to me."

That was some odd logic. I'd like her to be at least a little thankful to Halkara, since she'd done the cooking.

Fatla, by the way, was a little taken aback by Beelzebub's attitude. I guess it was shocking, since Fatla mostly saw Beelzebub at work.

"I must tip you for your service. Here, five thousand gold for each of you."

That was just a regular allowance! I came out from the kitchen to argue.

"Ma'am, I must ask that you not give my daughters allowance money, please."

"What? I will be paying for my meal as well. What's so wrong with this?"

"Elder Sister, can you pat my head? ♪"

"I told you! We don't offer those services!"

I was already getting tired dealing with Beelzebub, and Pecora was making it even worse.

"Wow, taking on both Boss and Her Majesty at once. You're sure having a time of it, huh, Azusa?"

Vania sure seemed proud of herself, for some reason. Fatla was the only one quietly eating her food.

"This is good. But my sister's cooking is much better," she said.

"Fatla, the girls and I are right here," I said. "You couldn't wait to insult the food?"

Scratch that—now Fatla was making unnecessary comments, too. I was well aware that Vania cooked on a professional level, so of course none of the family could compare…

When the girls left, Beelzebub and the rest of the demons finally started eating, and the café went quiet.

"What a handful…"

But while I was grabbing more orders, even weirder customers appeared.

A table had materialized where there wasn't one before. Sitting at it were Godly Godness and Nintan.

"We would like food, too. Two nectars, please."

"I'd love something ice-cold, please~"

"I know you don't have a numbered ticket. You can't be here—it's against the rules."

They weren't customers, so I didn't have to be polite to them.

"Numbered tickets are a system for mortals. Gods do not need them," Nintan said smugly. "And We brought this table Ourselves. Humans have no right to use it."

One piece of chop logic after another...

"There is no need to worry! The other customers cannot see our table."

"That's not the problem, Godly Godness. Bringing your own table to a café is grounds enough for a ban."

The next moment, the smug smile on Nintan's face grew even wider.

"The customer is god!"

I could tell she'd really wanted to say that. In fact, I bet that was the whole reason they came.

"I'm gonna bring over your menus super slowly... Or maybe I'll just pretend your order never went through to the kitchen..."

"Then I'll stick with the soda fountain~"

I wished she would stop bringing up things that didn't exist in this world. Obviously, we didn't have one of those.

Afterward, when I passed by the gods' table again, I found Ost Ande sitting with them. I guess that was better than more tables magically appearing...

Ost Ande was a little alien looking—she was basically a weird ball of hair—so it was better that no one could see her.

They were uninvited guests, but they were still guests, so I went to take their order.

"An author's not a real author until they have a favorite café... Oh, I would prefer to have nectar, please. An author must sometimes order things that are not on the menu. Though I would like you to officially add it in at some point in the future."

"I think you're a little too concerned about appearances..."

"I might make this my go-to café..."

"You'll have to get permission from the manager, who runs this place every other day of the year. I'll ask her for you while I'm in the kitchen."

I went to the back room, where Misjantie was doing some administrative stuff. Work like this suited her well, even if there was nothing pine-spirity about it.

"Uh, do we have nectar here?"

"Huh? That's not on the menu, man... Do we have a problem customer asking for things not on the menu? I'll go talk to one of the water spirits..."

"Sorry. Some of our customers are gods, you see."

Misjantie frowned. "I didn't think about gods visiting, man!"

"And the reaper is asking if it's okay for her to become a regular visitor."

"It'll be bad for business if word gets out that one of my regulars is the *reaper*! If I put a sign out front reading *This is the reaper's favorite spot!* it'll scare all the other regulars away!"

She was right. That'd be terrifying.

I didn't want to turn into a messenger girl, so I brought Misjantie to the gods' table.

"Uh, I'm really happy you swung by for a visit, man, but I don't really have anything I can offer a god... What? A café run by a spirit is already better than one run by a human? I guess so, but..."

This was supposed to be a conversation between three gods and a spirit, but there was nothing dignified or majestic about it at all.

I stepped back and turned to Flatorte, who was washing dishes.

"I guess you can't avoid trouble, even if you're only open for one day a year."

If anything, maybe it was guaranteed that something weird would happen, since all the pranksters would end up coming on the same day...

"Just ban the problem customers. That's the best you can do." A simple solution—very Flatorte-like.

"Blue dragons always get banned. If they don't want us around, then it's best if they just tell us that."

So she was a veteran!

Eventually, our acquaintances went home one by one.

I hadn't chased them out, though. They came in exceptionally early, so they naturally left early, too. Even the gods and their table had vanished at some point.

When Halkara's family left, she struck a little victory pose where the other customers couldn't see her. I think she'd *really* hated having them there.

We'd made it over the first hill, at last.

At one point, one of our normal customers very kindly said, "It's nice that the café is a little on the plain side this year."

"Thank you," I said.

My gratitude was genuine. I was so glad that what I was trying to accomplish was getting across. Relaxing but not too showy—that was the kind of café I wanted to run. Something cozy and out-of-the-way. If a café got too busy, it would only tire out both the customers and the staff.

"How wonderful, Lady Azusa."

Laika had come to wipe down the tables and had overheard the conversation.

"Yeah. I want our customers to relax, even if it's only for a short time."

Just then, the door opened. The next customer was here.

"Hello and welcome to the Witch's House Café!"

"Excuse me, but I'm an editor from the magazine *Café Friends Monthly*, and I'd like to interview Miss Laika!"

Word of Laika's popularity was spreading!

"Oh, um… I have to go help in the kitchen… Pardon me!"

Laika casually but hastily went straight to the back of the shop to hide.

"I do have a numbered ticket! I'll order something in the meantime, so please let me know when Laika is free for an interview."

Hmm, how was I supposed to handle this? Oh, I know.

I put on my customer service smile and said, "I'll go get the manager. Please wait there."

If a regular staff member couldn't fully resolve the situation, then it was time to rely on the manager! I had Misjantie come over straight away.

Please help, manager!

"Uhhh, hey, I'm the manager, man. Sorry, but you've gotta notify us beforehand if you want an interview. Otherwise I dunno if we can accept. The staff aren't expecting interviews, see. But you're free to write down what you think of the café as a whole while you use our services. Go ahead, man. Oh, and please don't wait for the workday to be over and approach our employees while they're leaving the café. That just increases their work time. Thanks for your understanding, man."

Our manager was handling this with surprising professionalism…

There *were* some customers here primarily to see Laika, but it seemed like we'd get through this without any major problems. Laika, however, blushed every time someone looked at her.

"P-please call me over wh-when you've decided on your order!"

Gosh, she was so cute. I was a staff member, and I still saw her as our poster girl.

Incidentally, whenever a customer said, "Laika's so cute!" the manager came running.

"Excuse me, please don't tease our employees, man. Our establishment's aim is only to offer its customers a relaxing time."

It seemed our manager was ready to properly defend her employees.

Back in the employee area, Laika murmured, "I'll have to thank our manager this year. She's been a huge help."

"Yeah. You're right," I said.

Laika had already started calling Misjantie her manager.

And so despite a few problems (mostly caused by customers), the Witch's House Café reached closing time, and the last group of patrons went home.

"Come again! We only help out once annually, but the House of the Pine Spirit is open all year round!"

Once the door closed, I turned around. The staff—my family—were all gathered together.

"A job well done, Lady Azusa! It is finally over... I can catch my breath at last."

"You look like you've just finished a marathon, Laika. I'm proud of you."

"Next time, I want to swap duties with Flatorte..."

"You'll have to talk to Flatorte about that..."

Flatorte, incidentally, had been carrying in ingredients and doing the cleaning. The reason why she had been restricted to working in the back was because of her manners, which left a little to be desired.

"I, the great blue dragon Flatorte, refuse to bow to the customer's whims. I'd freeze those arrogant ingrates."

"...You see what we're working with? We don't want anyone to get hurt. I hope you understand."

"Yes. We cannot have that... I suppose I will just have to bear the embarrassment."

Sandra must have been exhausted. She looked like she had been sleeping, but now that everything was finished, Falfa and Shalsha had woken her up and brought her over.

"Shalsha feels more confident in her work this year."

"Falfa did so well at calculating the bills!"

"Yes, both of you did wonderfully!" I said. "And, Sandra, you behaved very well."

Sandra had done her job, too, albeit in her own way. As her mom, I'd been keeping a quiet eye on her.

"Well, I don't mind working for you every once in a while," she said. "I'd be a good-for-nothing if I sat around photosynthesizing all day."

I got the feeling her response meant she was happier than she let on.

Meanwhile, the moment work finished, Halkara had started drinking booze out of a glass.

"Ahhh. Drinks after work taste the best! In fact, they're pretty good even when I haven't done anything!"

"Halkara! You were just waiting to pull that out, weren't you?! Well, as long as you weren't drinking during work, I guess it's fine…"

There had been bumps along the way, but overall the café was a success.

Misjantie emerged from the back, joining us.

"I've been watching you guys work today, and I learned a lot, man. I hope to put it all to use during the rest of the year."

"I'm not sure it'll be much help, but we'll leave it in your hands, Manager."

"I'll have the priests working tomorrow come in early and clean up, so you all go home and rest, man."

It seemed like the priests weren't so much priests anymore as café employees. But that was a problem for the pine spirit and her temple, so I decided to let it go.

"Let's rest up tonight, and tomorrow, we can go enjoy the Dance Festival."

Falfa was already getting excited about the stalls we'd see, despite the huge line of them we'd seen today stretching all the way from Flatta to Nascúte (thanks to the demons)… That said, it was probably going to be a lot livelier in Flatta the next day.

On the way home, I bought an outfit from Nosonia. The items at Canhein's stall weren't that appealing, so I didn't get anything. *Sorry, Canhein.*

◇

The day of the Dance Festival had finally arrived, and the whole family attended.

There were more markets and stalls throughout Flatta than there had been the day before. One of the stall holders was Eno, the Witch of the Grotto and Halkara's business competitor.

"You're already so popular. I'm impressed you're still out here putting in the work yourself," I said to Eno, who was minding the stall.

"There are things one can only see standing behind the booth, you know. There is a lot you can't learn just acting as manager at a factory." As she finished speaking, Eno's gaze turned to Halkara.

"Gosh, well, Halkara Pharmaceuticals has to send products all over the country, so we need to operate at a pretty large scale. But I see that as my mission in society. Of course, I don't expect those not in the know to understand~"

"But you don't get to see your customers when you mass-produce products, do you?"

"Hmm? Is that slander I hear? Would you like me to sue you?"

Can't they call a cease-fire for the festival, at least?

I had a feeling Eno and Halkara hated each other precisely because they were so similar, but I knew they would both turn their ire on me if I said as much, so I kept my mouth shut.

Besides, there was something more important than the stalls. In the center of town, everyone was dancing away, making up their own moves. That's right—today, we would dance. Nothing else mattered.

"Big Sis, I had the same thought last year, but everyone's rhythms and moves are all different. Is that how it's supposed to be?" Rosalie asked me. She was right—the dancers had nothing in common, except that they were all moving.

"Yeah. No one's worried about things like that. All you have to do is move. As long as no one gets hurt, it's fine."

Falfa and Halkara had already joined the dancing circle and were moving however they pleased.

"Feel free to join in, Rosalie. Or you can just sit back and watch."

Shalsha was doing just that. She held Sandra's hand as they stood, motionless. I wasn't so keen on joining in, either.

"You're right. I'm already dead, so there's no point in feeling embarrassed. Maybe I'll join in. It's been a while anyway."

Rosalie made her way toward the circle, moving her hands around. I could tell she was getting into it, and her expression was softening, too.

"Hey, this isn't too hard, and it's a lot of fun!" she said.

I was glad she was enjoying herself. With stuff like this, all it took was moving your body to start having fun.

But then things started to go south—a peaceful expression crossed Rosalie's face, and she started floating into the air!

"This is so much fun! I'm having the time of my not-life! I'm so happy that I think I've found peace!"

"Wait, Rosalie! Stop, stop!" I called out in a panic.

"Whoa, that was close! I almost ascended! I was only dancing…"

It wasn't like we were at some temple listening to sermons of gratitude or something.

"Miss Rosalie, this Dance Festival was originally a folk event meant to soothe the spirits of the dead. It must have worked on you, since you are a spirit," Shalsha explained.

It was like the Bon festival in Japan…

"I see… I gotta be careful even when I dance. And now that I look around, it seems there aren't a lot of ghosts here today…"

Maybe they had already found peace. I supposed that was a good thing if it was what they wanted.

"There are lots of ways to enjoy a festival, Rosalie. You just have to breathe in the atmosphere…"

"Yeah… It's nice listening to the music, too."

She was right—music was being played to accompany the dancing, and I could hear singing from the stage.

However, just then, I heard something that caught my attention.

"The next one to sing for us will be Kuku the almiraj!"

As the audience clapped, Kuku stepped onto the stage, lute on her back. Kuku's performances were becoming a regular thing for us now. I was worried... I could only imagine she would play a sad song and dampen the mood of the festival...

"Hello!" she said. "I'm going to work my hardest to make sure this festival's a blast! So please listen to this next song, 'If We're All Going to Die Anyway'!"

The name alone was super depressing!

But Kuku knew what was going on here. The lyrics were about how if we were all going to die anyway, then we should party hard. The tune was upbeat and perfect to dance to.

"Looks like Kuku made some changes."

"She may have reflected on what happened at the relay race... Back then, even I felt despondent..."

Apparently, everyone remembered the disaster at the relay race...

"I've been seeing so many people since yesterday. I was concerned someone might be plotting something this year, but I guess I've been worried for nothing."

"You should not say such things, Lady Azusa..." Laika seemed uncomfortable.

She must be worried I've jinxed it...

Then, for some reason, Laika wrapped her arms around herself.

"I just felt a terrible chill," she said. "I think something is coming..."

"Coming? What's coming? Your family?"

Halkara's family had come by, so I wouldn't be surprised if Laika's family did the same.

"No, that would not give me chills. Something much more wicked approaches... Or so my instincts tell me."

I was wondering what it could be, when all of a sudden, the sky was blocked out. Clouds?

I looked up to see a whole mass of dragons above us—and they were all blue dragons!

"What's this? Flatorte's family? No, there's way too many of them..."

"Do you know what is happening, Flatorte?" Laika turned to her, furious.

"I honestly have no idea what's going on! They might just be passing through."

But they weren't. The blue dragons began to take on human form and descend upon the Dance Festival.

"Seriously, what is going on?" I asked. "Flatorte, are you sure you aren't involved in some fight?"

"Please, do such things in your own village...," said Laika. "If you lose control here, Flatta will be destroyed."

"I, Flatorte, am innocent! I have no idea what's going on!"

Even if that was true, this gang of dragons might remember something she didn't... Depending on how the situation shook out, I might have to step in before anyone was hurt. I really didn't want to fight on a festival day with so many people around, but I didn't exactly have a choice if disaster broke out.

The blue dragons went straight for the plaza in the middle of town—the center of the festivities.

Please don't do anything... They were in their human forms, so I didn't think they would start breathing ice all over everything, but I was still concerned.

And then all at once—

—they started dancing.

"They're just here to dance?!"

It seemed they had no ill intentions and were simply dancing away in silence.

What's more, only some of the blue dragons were dancing. Others were off buying great amounts of meat skewers and trying all the food the event had to offer.

As the blue dragons passed by, I heard some of them speaking.

"Man, festivals are great!" "I always get so excited!" "I'm gonna use every last coin to my name today!"

"It seems like they're just here for the festival," I said.

Laika looked exhausted, probably from the tension. She was often the blue dragons' target.

"It appears so," she said. "But why come all this way...?"

It seemed not even one of the dragons had business with Flatorte.

As Shalsha watched them dance, she said, "Those who live unprincipled lives typically cut loose on festival days. The less interest a festival-goer has in the event's origins, the rowdier they tend to act."

"Just like a pack of delinquents!"

Now that I thought about it, I remembered seeing guys with rough hairstyles partying it up on festival days in my past life. It seemed blue dragons and festivals went well together.

"But Flatta is so far away from the blue dragon village. Is something like this worth coming all this way?"

Laika had a point. This wasn't their local festival. Could word of the Dance Festival have spread that far?

"Mistress, blue dragons don't think deeply about such things," Flatorte explained. "Someone probably mentioned there was a festival out this way and suggested they all go, and anyone looking for something to do came along. That's all. And the majority of blue dragons are always looking for something to do."

"That sounds about right," I said.

It would be weirder if everything had a clear and logical reason behind it. Whimsically deciding to go to a festival you just happened to hear about sounded like a perfectly good way to live.

The blue dragons joined Falfa and Halkara on the dance floor.

"Hey, kiddos. Where do you live?" a blue dragon-girl asked.

"Near the village!" Falfa announced.

"I see. It's nice and cool here. I'm gonna get meat after this; you want some?"

It seemed she had an unexpected soft spot for kids.

I felt like Flatta's Dance Festival had descended into chaos these past few years, but no one was getting hurt, so I guessed it was okay. Besides, a festival was exactly the time to let loose and party.

I wanted to tell Falfa not to go off with strangers, but the blue dragon-girl was a friend of Flatorte's, so I decided to let it slide this time.

"Looks like the Dance Festival will end on a nice note again this year," I said.

"Ugh! They haven't gone home yet?!"

My sentiments were immediately drowned out by Halkara's disgusted yell. I followed her gaze to see her entire family, drunk. In a way, the apple didn't fall far from the tree.

Halkara hadn't drunk at all that day, for a change, and I was one hundred percent sure it was because of her family.

A little while after the Dance Festival, Natalie from the guild came by the house in the highlands. Everyone else was either in their rooms or out shopping, so Flatorte and I welcomed her.

"Thank you all so much!" she said. "This is a letter of thanks from the mayor. And here's one from the province. Due to administrative reasons, it took some time to come through. My apologies."

Natalie handed me some parchment.

"It'd be rude of me to turn these down, so I'll take them, but why is the province sending me a letter of thanks…?"

Flatta might be under its administration, but I hadn't spoken to any employees of the province.

"There were a lot of shops lined up on the side of the road, helping to revitalize the region, so this is thanks for that."

I was pretty sure the demons did all that on their own... But it wasn't like I was receiving money for it, so I figured it was okay to accept the thank-you.

"By the way, how were things on the day of the festival?" I asked. "I was just a regular attendee this year."

I had tried to keep a low profile, both to avoid embarrassment and because I didn't want to turn the Dance Festival into something else.

"Oh, it was a great success! I have a feeling it may lead to a greater tax yield for the village!" Natalie replied enthusiastically.

"I see, I see. The region's benefiting, then... Oh, and there weren't any weird incidents or accidents, were there? It seemed like a lot of people came from all over the place."

It wouldn't do for me to get specific about some of the guests, so I stayed purposely vague. I *definitely* couldn't mention that the reaper had shown up. I didn't want people thinking the festival was cursed.

"Oh, well, if I had to say, some of those people calling themselves blue dragons got into a big argument at the tavern."

Oh, crap! I hope they didn't make a mess of the place!

"But they simply said, 'Fine, then! I'll meet you at the iceberg!' 'Fine. You better not chicken out on the way, punk!' and left, so the tavern itself was fine."

"They were going to fight it out on an iceberg...?"

Better that than simply "taking it outside," I supposed. More ice on an iceberg shouldn't be a problem.

"That sounds like them, all right. They fight over the littlest things," said Flatorte, our representative of blue dragonkind. It might be bad to judge a book by its cover, but it seemed blue dragons were indeed quick to resort to violence.

"What were they arguing over anyway?"

"It was apparently over who would pay."

"Oh, so they were like, 'You pay!' 'No, you pay'?"

They had all seemed kind of broke.

"No, Great Witch, quite the opposite. They were apparently yelling, 'I'll pay!' 'No, I'll pay!' to one another."

"They could have just split the bill!"

Now I had the feeling they were only inventing reasons to fight.

"Mistress, blue dragons place a lot of importance on saving face. Letting someone else pay for you means acknowledging them as your superior, so it's hard to step down."

"I get it, but that's why they should split the bill evenly."

"But if you split the bill, then the others will think you're stingy because you don't want to pay for everything. So that won't work, either."

The world of saving face was fraught with peril.

"I guess it's fine, so long as no buildings in the village were destroyed. I hope the Dance Festival stays peaceful from here on out. Anything else, Natalie?"

"Oh yes. The House of the Pine Spirit has made some changes, and they're being very well received."

"A change? This is the first I'm hearing about it…"

Maybe they'd gotten an idea or two after watching us work.

"I've been once, and the walk was totally worth it. You should go in the morning next time you have the chance!"

And so in response to Natalie's suggestion, the whole family went to the House of the Pine Spirit (though I asked Rosalie and Sandra to stay behind). Luckily, due to the location, Halkara could go straight to work in Nascúte.

There was nothing different about the pine tree tunnel, only a sign on one of the trunks that read OPEN. The atmosphere made me think of a very stylish out-of-the-way café, and I could tell that's what they were going for.

But right at the entrance stood a new, much bigger sign.

"Lady Azusa, I suppose this means they are offering a breakfast set. But all day? Wouldn't that no longer be considered breakfast…?" Laika asked—a reasonable question.

"I have a bad feeling about this…," I said. "Let's just go inside."

When we entered, one of the priests took us to an empty table.

I'd gotten thirsty just from the walk, so I decided to order tea for all of us first.

"Mistress, I'm hungry. I want to order food, too. I haven't had any breakfast yet, so I need more than just tea."

"I know how you feel, Flatorte. But sit tight. There's something I want to check."

The waiter immediately brought us the tea, as well as several plates loaded with things that were definitely not tea.

"Here's your tea—along with breakfast toast, salad, hard-boiled eggs, cheese, fruit, and nuts."

"That sure is a lot of extras!"

"Wow~ What a deal! We only ordered tea, and a complete breakfast came with it! ♪ I should come here before I go to work at the factory."

"Personally, I could use a bit more toast," said Laika. "But it does make me happy that all of this came with the tea."

The family was naturally delighted. Falfa and Shalsha dug in to their café breakfast right away.

This was certainly no problem. In fact, the scene was a treat for the eyes. But there was one thing I couldn't help wondering about.

"I'm going to talk to Misjantie for a quick second."

I went to find her in the back.

"What other dishes should I add, man…? Oh! Hi, Azusa."

"Misjantie, what prompted you to add the breakfast set?"

I already had a good idea, however.

"Oh, that. The night after you took over the shop, I received an oracle from a goddess telling me to add a breakfast set to morning tea because it'd be a big hit, man."

I knew Godly Godness was involved!

"I thought it'd be a huge money sink including all those extras, but a whole bunch of people started coming once we added it to the menu. We're turning a profit, man!"

All it would take was a little inspiration to come up with something like this, and it wasn't all that strange. But I knew this kind of service was part of the culture of the Nagoya-Gifu region of Japan, and so I suspected it might be Godly Godness's way of offering her thanks after arriving without warning.

I returned to the table to find Laika eating spaghetti off a hot griddle.

"Lady Azusa, this noodle dish is quite good! There's even an egg underneath the spaghetti!"

That was a Nagoya thing, too. This café was going to take a very original path to success—I was sure of it.

The End

※ This story is an edited version of the script of the first drama CD, contained in the special release edition of Volume 5.

SCENE 0

AZUSA – NARRATION
I'm Azusa, also known as the Witch of the Highlands. I look like a high school girl, but my life has been three hundred years of killing slimes and making potions.

These days, I've been living with Laika, a dragon girl, Falfa and Shalsha, my daughters, who are also slime spirits, and Halkara, a troublemaker elf.

An important demon by the name of Beelzebub seems to have taken a liking to me, and she comes to visit a lot, too.

Anyway, at the foot of the highlands where we live is a little village called Flatta. Today marked the end of an event called the Dance Festival being held there… A lot of stuff happened, and we ended up walking around in maid outfits.

It was a huge success, but it was kind of embarrassing… In any case, the festival ended, and we all came home to the house in the highlands.

SCENE 1

AZUSA
Phew! Another Flatta Dance Festival in the bag.
LAIKA
Lady Azusa, those frilly outfits do really wear me out...
AZUSA
The villagers were really fussing over you, weren't they? Well, it only happens once a year, so you'll be fine.
LAIKA
Does that mean we will be doing the Witch's House Café again next year?
AZUSA
I guess that depends on how things go. But it seems like the villagers are hoping we will.
FALFA
Mommy! Falfa can't wait for next year's Dance Festival!
SHALSHA
We cannot turn back time, but these sorts of functions make it appear to repeat in yearly cycles. Shalsha is also very deeply interested.
AZUSA
Shalsha, I'm afraid I'm not really following.
FALFA
What Shalsha's saying, Mommy, is that she wants to do it again next year, too!
AZUSA
Thanks for interpreting, Falfa. You're right. It's kind of fun to play restaurateur once every year. Let's try to do the Witch's House Café again next time if we can.

HALKARA
Ahhh. Festival day is a great time for booze!
AZUSA
You're already drunk, Halkara. Look at you; you can barely walk. I'm surprised you made it back to the house.
HALKARA
Oh, come on. I've barely had anything to drink... Eee... Heh-heh... Ah-ha-ha-ha!
AZUSA
You're not gonna barf again, are you...?
HALKARA
Please, Madam Teacher, I think I've learned a thing or two from—I'm...I'm going to the bathroom!
AZUSA
See? I knew this would happen! You run a pharmaceuticals company, so you ought to take better care of yourself!
BEELZEBUB
She never changes. 'Tis hard to change one's personality after reaching adulthood.
AZUSA
That's true. But, Beelzebub, why are you still here? I mean, you can stay if you want, but don't you have work?
BEELZEBUB
I took off through tomorrow, so I will be fine. I like to put in for a day or so extra vacation after events like these so I can fully relax.
AZUSA
You're right. It's hard to go right back to work the day after a party. Though you can't do that unless your job allows you to take the time.

BEELZEBUB

We demons place great emphasis on worker satisfaction.

AZUSA

Demons sure are advanced when it comes to that stuff. Anyway, I guess that means we'll need food for six people tomorrow.

BEELZEBUB

Very well. Then I shall cook for you tomorrow morning! That will allow you to relax, no? 'Tis repayment for allowing me to stay at your house.

AZUSA

I see. That's not a bad compromise.

BEELZEBUB

I shall prepare for you the greatest breakfast ever. You'd best be ready for it.

FALFA

Falfa will help!

SHALSHA

Shalsha is curious about demon cooking. I want to watch.

BEELZEBUB

Oh? You'll both help me? How that warms my heart. You two are so pure!

AZUSA

Oh no! What if Beelzebub takes my kids away from me? How am I supposed to relax…?

LAIKA

Lady Azusa, do you have a moment?

AZUSA

Aww, I knew you'd stay with me, at least. You really are like my little sister!

LAIKA

…Miss Halkara is acting like the living dead in the bathroom, so I need your help caring for her.

AZUSA
Oh, that. Right, I'll help. That's what family is for, after all…

SCENE 2

Azusa and Laika head to the bathroom, where Halkara is.

AZUSA
You're as white as a sheet.
HALKARA
Wh-why did I drink so much…?
AZUSA
I'd like to ask you the same thing.
HALKARA
The alcohol is like my lover when I'm drinking it, but now it's like a terrible, terrible bandit…
AZUSA
It's incredible that someone who makes potions for a living understands so little about their own body…
LAIKA
I believe Miss Halkara lacks self-control. Why don't you join me in training every morning? It will temper your spirit.
HALKARA
Sorry, but no thank you.
LAIKA
You might learn to breathe fire from your mouth.
AZUSA
No, she won't. And even if she did, she'd just get drunk and burn something down. So please don't encourage her.

* * *

AZUSA – NARRATION
And so the night after the festival ended peacefully… Well, not for Halkara, but that was her own fault, so it doesn't count.

Sound of water boiling.

BEELZEBUB
Cooking is heat! Cooking is explosions! Cooking is tears!
FALFA
Whoa! Look at the color! It's all pitch-black!
SHALSHA
Just what I would expect from a demon. The aroma in my nostrils holds a unique appeal. No, this is more of a stench.

AZUSA – NARRATION
I heard terrible things happening in the kitchen. An awful feeling was forming in my stomach. Were we going to be okay tomorrow…?

SCENE 3

Birds chirping.

AZUSA
Yaaawn… Good morning.
FALFA
Oh, Mommy! Good morning! This is our breakfast today!

SHALSHA

It came out magnificently. Very tasty. You must eat it, too, Mom.

AZUSA

Those are two major seals of approval. What a relief.

BEELZEBUB

You were thinking rude things about me, weren't you? I take this very seriously, you know. Try the acidic swamp bread!

AZUSA

I'm glad you're so confident, but I can't say that sounds very appetizing. Though…it does *look* tasty. We called this deep-fried bread in my past life. That deep amber color is making me hungry.

BEELZEBUB

I know not of your past life, but now is the time to eat up. As we demons say, there is nothing more boring than talking about one's food before eating it.

AZUSA

I see. I guess that makes sense. Here goes nothing.

Sounds of munching on bread.

AZUSA

O-oh my god. This is…this is so good! The outer shell is a crispy, crunchy texture, but it's so moist on the inside! And it's stuffed full of veggies and meats, and the inside isn't soggy! The spices are tickling my nose!

FALFA

Yes! Mommy likes it! Falfa helped stir-fry the vegetables!

SHALSHA

As a participant in this endeavor, Shalsha is glad to have her hard work pay off.

BEELZEBUB

Aye, indeed. The girls did wonderfully.

AZUSA

Hey, hold on. Stop calling them "the girls."

BEELZEBUB

What? They are girls, so that is what one should call them.

AZUSA

When you say it, it sounds like you're secretly trying to make them *your* girls... I am never, ever, ever letting you adopt Falfa or Shalsha, all right?

BEELZEBUB

More importantly, tell me what you think of the bread. I am not going to abduct the girls.

AZUSA

This is *definitely* curry bread! And it's perfect, like a model example.

BEELZEBUB

Do not name my food. This is acidic swamp bread. 'Twas named after the stinging sensation of an acidic swamp, and 'tis a perfectly respectable demon delicacy.

AZUSA

C'mon, that doesn't sound tasty at all. But I'm serious; I've had bread like this before. It was called curry bread, because there was a spicy stew called curry, except with all the watery bits drained out, inside a bread roll.

BEELZEBUB

Oh-ho. That sounds a bit like demon curreh. What is inside acidic swamp bread is close to curreh.

AZUSA

Oh, so you have curry, too.

BEELZEBUB
No, no. Not curry. *Curreh.* Curreh, Azusa.
AZUSA
You're really picky about that pronunciation.
BEELZEBUB
'Tis its name. One does not pronounce it *curry* even in the most dire of circumstances.
AZUSA
Fine. This isn't going anywhere, so I'll leave it at that.

The door opens.

LAIKA
Good morning.
HALKARA
Ooh… I'm so hungover… There's a bull on a rampage in my skull…
AZUSA
Morning, you two. Come here and try Beelzebub's curry bread.
BEELZEBUB
'Tis acidic swamp bread! How many times do I have to—? Oh, forget it. Give it a taste.

Sounds of munching on bread.

LAIKA
Oh! This is quite delicious!
HALKARA
It is! But…I have heartburn right now. I wish I could have some when I'm feeling better…
BEELZEBUB
That is not my problem.

AZUSA

Oh yeah. I want to make curry...I mean curreh. Do you have a recipe, Beelzebub? I should be able to make some acidic swamp bread as long as I have the ingredients.

FALFA

Oh! You're not supposed to do that!

SHALSHA

Yes. Shalsha heard the same from Miss Beelzebub.

AZUSA

Oh? What are you two talking about?

BEELZEBUB

Oh-ho-ho. The inside of this bread is similar to curreh, yes. But the filling has been simplified so that it may be put inside the bread roll. If you wish to make curreh itself, then you must get your hands on quite a number of valuable spices. Otherwise, it is not true curreh.

AZUSA

Oh, it doesn't have to be that authentic. It can just be average.

BEELZEBUB

Absolutely not. I do not wish to cook a pale imitation of curreh and leave you with a false impression! At the very least, we'll need bab nuts and hacko herbs and anima leaves... Well, I suppose I could cook it for you if you brought me the ingredients.

AZUSA

I'll pass. That's too much work.

BEELZEBUB

I would *cook* it for you if you *brought* me the *ingredients*!

AZUSA

Ah. It wasn't optional.

* * *

AZUSA – NARRATION
And so, by bringing the subject up first, I painted myself into a corner and ended up searching for each of the spices. We made a whole occasion out of it, and I went looking for the bab nuts with Laika, the hacko herbs with Falfa and Shalsha, and the anima leaves with Halkara.

SCENE 4

Rustling grass.

AZUSA – NARRATION
First, Laika took her dragon form and flew me to the faraway habitat of bab nuts.

AZUSA
Sorry for dragging you all the way out here. The fault is half Beelzebub's and half mine.
LAIKA
Oh, I don't mind. In a way, this is just more herb gathering, like for your medicines. And...I am happy I have the chance to work alone with you, Lady Azusa...
AZUSA
Aw, thanks. I'm glad to hear it.
LAIKA
This is a very thick forest, though. I keep tripping over the vines.
AZUSA
Me too. These bab nuts are apparently very

special tree nuts. I had no idea they were also used to make spices.

LAIKA
What are they like?

AZUSA
They're okay when they're dry, but while fresh, they tend to affect the mental state of animals.

LAIKA
Like narcotics?

AZUSA
Oh, nothing that dangerous. They're not addictive, either. But they can cause temporary age regression.

LAIKA
Age regression…?

AZUSA
Yeah. It apparently makes you want to cling like a baby to the nearest person. I've heard it's especially effective on typically serious people, so be careful not to step on any, okay?

LAIKA
I see. But I train my spirit constantly, so I am confident I'll be able to overcome it.

AZUSA
That's true. You might be able to manage. But just in case, watch where you step.

LAIKA
I will. Oh—!!!

A *crunch* as Laika steps on something.

AZUSA
Hmm? What's wrong?! Was there a snake? Though I guess snakes aren't that scary for a dragon.

LAIKA

I'm sorry. It appears I stepped on some sort of nut...

AZUSA

Oh, that's probably a bab nut... Try not to inhale its scent too mu— Laika? Why do you look like you're going to cry?

Laika experiences age regression.

LAIKA

Lady Azusa...I...I...feel helpless...

AZUSA

Oh no. Have you regressed...?

LAIKA

I am always enjoying myself living in the house in the highlands, and so I never think about it, but...um... I suddenly remembered that I'm living away from my parents...

AZUSA

Oh, you're homesick. That's perfectly normal.

LAIKA

Waaaaaah! Waaaaaah! I'm sad! And scared!

AZUSA

Whoa, whoa! Don't cry, don't cry! There's nothing to be afraid of! I'm right here. It's okay, it's okay.

LAIKA

Your smell calms me down, Big Sis...

AZUSA

I'm your big sister? Well...I suppose that's fine. Yes, your big sister Azusa's going to take good care of you. There's nothing to fear. There, there. Good girl. You're a good kid, Laika. That's it.

LAIKA

Rub my back, Big Sis...

AZUSA
………Okay.

Azusa rubs Laika's back.

AZUSA
How's that? Are you a little calmer now? If there's anything bothering you, you can tell me everything, okay? You're always so good, Laika. You can depend on me all you want today. I…don't think I want this to go on for days, but the bab nut's effects shouldn't be that strong.

LAIKA
Thank you, Big Sis. You're so warm.

AZUSA
Am I? I'm glad.

LAIKA
Big Sis, let me rest my head on your lap.

AZUSA
Wow, those bab nuts sure are something. She keeps asking for more… But I guess I don't really mind. All right, come put your head on your big sister Azusa's lap.

LAIKA
Thank you. I feel so safe here… I'm not lonely, even without my family…

AZUSA
I see. Well, we know where the nuts are, so we can take our time. You can always rely on me if you need to.

LAIKA
…Um, can I ask you something?

AZUSA
Sure, sure. Of course. Anything you like.

LAIKA
Will I ever be as wonderful as you…?
AZUSA
Is that what you're worried about?
LAIKA
You've spent so long slowly killing slimes and building up your accomplishments… Could I ever stick to one thing for such a long time…?
AZUSA
Of course you can. After all, you're *my* little sister, Laika!
LAIKA
M-maybe…
AZUSA
Trust me.
LAIKA
All right. I'll try…
AZUSA
Good. But you don't have to try anything right now. Just rest.

Time passes.

AZUSA
………She fell asleep. I guess spending time like this isn't so bad every once in a while. I just hope she doesn't sleep for so long that my legs start to hurt.

Time passes. Laika wakes up.

LAIKA
Aaaah! What have I done?!
AZUSA
Oh, you're awake. Good morning, Laika.

LAIKA

I'm so sorry! It seems I was acting in a very embarrassing manner with you because of that bab nut... I'm sorry, I'm so sorry!

AZUSA

You don't have to apologize. More importantly, was Big Sis Azusa's lap comfortable?

LAIKA

L-Lady Azusa... Please do not tease me so... I am not the sort of person to lean on others that way... Ohh, just recalling it makes me want to spit flame!

AZUSA

Most people would just turn red from embarrassment, but you can actually produce fire. Please be careful. We don't want to burn the forest down.

LAIKA

I-I'll try...

AZUSA

I'm actually happy I got to hear some of what you feel deep inside. It does get a little lonely living so far away from your family, doesn't it?

LAIKA

W-well, maybe... But only sometimes...

AZUSA

You still feel it, though. I'm not much of a replacement, but if you need someone to lean on, then you're more than welcome to come to me. I know it might be embarrassing in the house, but it's not a problem out here.

LAIKA

.........Um, then could you rub my head and back one more time...?

AZUSA

I'll do whatever my cute little sister asks! Come over here.

LAIKA
A-all right... One day, I will pay you back for all the guidance you have given me...
AZUSA
It's nothing, really.

AZUSA – NARRATION
I doted on Laika plenty during her age regression, and it was actually pretty nice. And we got our bab nuts, too.

SCENE 5

AZUSA – NARRATION
This time, I joined my daughters on dragon Laika's back around noontime, and we went to the fields in search of hacko herbs. We figured Laika would be tired, so we let her rest while we searched.

FALFA
Wooow! Look how big the plain is!
AZUSA
Now, Falfa, don't run too fast, or you'll trip.
SHALSHA
The land stretches on as far as the eye can see. What a perfect place for contemplation. Now I can see just how small and insignificant I am. This will surely lead me to true self-knowledge.
AZUSA
Shalsha, please, don't just plop down and start meditating... Couldn't you be a little more like a

kid…? You can run around in the grass, you know? You two are such polar opposites.

FALFA

What kind of plant is the hacko herb anyway?

AZUSA

It grows among the other grasses and sprouts purple flowers. It doesn't care one bit about fitting in, so just look for the purple flowers.

SHALSHA

Purple is a noble color. This plant must be very aloof.

AZUSA

That seems to be the case. Oh, and try not to breathe in the pollen. It has a very slight hallucinogenic effect.

FALFA

Okay! Falfa is a good girl, so I'll do as you say!

SHALSHA

What sort of hallucinogenic effects, Mom?

AZUSA

It's weak, so adults don't tend to notice anything, but children grow oddly rebellious. They start acting like the hacko herb, like they're immune to the influences of others.

FALFA

Hmm. But Falfa will never have a rebellious phase. Because Falfa loves you, Mommy!

AZUSA

I know. And I hope that never changes!

SHALSHA

A rebellious phase… Shalsha doesn't really understand, but Shalsha won't steal any wyverns.

AZUSA

Stealing a wyvern sounds pretty difficult.

SHALSHA

Others experiencing a rebellious phase apparently smash stained-glass windows in churches.

AZUSA

That sounds more like something a villain would do.

Sounds of insects and rustling grass.

FALFA

Hacko herb, where are you? Where are you, hacko herb?

SHALSHA

Perhaps this is one of those times where we eventually learn it was right beside us all along. And so Shalsha looks next to us and finds…nothing.

AZUSA

It's apparently somewhat rare. But we can take our time searching, like we're out on a picnic. You know, I'm having a lot of fun spending time in the sun with both of you.

FALFA

Where are you, hacko herb? Hello? Oh! A stink bug!

AZUSA

Those can get very stinky, so don't touch it!

SHALSHA

Shalsha is sleepy.

AZUSA

Shalsha, try to keep searching for just a little longer, okay? Hmm, this might take more time than I thought.

* * *

Time passes.

FALFA
Mommy, Falfa put a flower in her hair!
SHALSHA
Mom, Shalsha has adorned herself with a flower.
AZUSA
Oh! Look how cute you both are! That purple flower is so pretty on you! ………Wait, purple?
FALFA
Oh, is this the hacko herb?
SHALSHA
Plants do not know their own names. Yet they still produce beautiful flowers.
AZUSA
You found them! Nice work, you two!
FALFA
This flower smells so nice!
SHALSHA
Plants do not know their own names. Yet they still produce such lovely scents.
AZUSA
Wait, you're both smelling it…? You're not going to rebel on me, are you…?

Falfa and Shalsha enter their rebellious phase.

FALFA
……Mommy, Falfa hates these kiddie clothes. I want a shorter skirt.
AZUSA
Falfa? What are you talking about?
SHALSHA
Shalsha thinks studying is boring and pointless.

I am going to live life without thought to any damage I cause; I will do what I please with no thought to the future. Let the cards fall as they may. Shalsha will skip studying today and tomorrow.

AZUSA

You, too, Shalsha?! I guess the hacko herb's effects are real...

FALFA

Shalsha, let's stop looking for this stupid herb and get some water at the tavern.

SHALSHA

Understood. Only the tavern can soothe our souls.

AZUSA

No! You're way too young for that! Stop talking like delinquents! ...Though I guess if it's only water, it's not that big a deal.

FALFA

Move, Mommy. Falfa hates this boring stuff.

SHALSHA

Shalsha feels somehow compelled to turn my back on what my parent says.

AZUSA

Oh no! They're both taking the wrong path in life! Quick, change back to normal! Mommy's going to cry!

FALFA

Whatever. Falfa hates you.

SHALSHA

Children are supposed to make their parents cry.

AZUSA

Falfa said she hates me... Falfa's rebelling and saying she hates me... Even if it's all because of the hacko herb, it's still a shock... Seeing them try to act grown-up is frankly pretty cute, but it's a shock, too...

FALFA

Hmph. Falfa's a bad girl! When Falfa gets home, I'm going to cut my skirts short and chase grasshoppers!

AZUSA

Ohh… She can't bring herself to go full delinquent. How adorable!

SHALSHA

Shalsha is going to the library to read lots of antiestablishment philosophy books.

AZUSA

Ohh… And Shalsha's just as studious as ever. So precious!

FALFA

Okay, well, Falfa and Shalsha are going home first. Let's go, Shalsha.

SHALSHA

Wait a second.

FALFA

What is it, Shalsha?

SHALSHA

Shalsha wants to rebel, but…I also feel guilty leaving Mom behind… We're still children… We still use our parent's money to eat, even when we're rebelling… Such rebellion is not genuine…

AZUSA

Ah, she's fallen into that familiar dilemma, where a delinquent realizes they're being supported by the very people they're resisting.

FALFA

Hey, that's not fair, Shalsha… Falfa…feels guilty, too… It's not like I blame Mommy…

AZUSA

Ohh, I can't stand it! You're both so cute! It's like seasoning food with salt to draw out the sweetness! I'm going to hug both of you!

FALFA
Ugh, Mommy! You're squeezing too tight!
SHALSHA
We're supposed to be rebelling...
AZUSA
My love for you won't change, even if you rebel! And I know you love me very much!

Falfa and Shalsha start crying.

FALFA
I'm sorry, Mommy! I love you, Mommy!
SHALSHA
I gave in to the hallucination. I'm sorry, Mom...
AZUSA
Oh, I'm so glad! You're back to normal! Mommy's so happy!

AZUSA – NARRATION
My daughters went through a little delinquent phase, but we successfully got our hacko herbs. When they were trying to be bad, my girls were still so precious. Even if they go through the real thing one day, I think we'll be all right.

SCENE 6

AZUSA – NARRATION
Finally, I went searching for the leaves of the anima tree with Halkara. I had a feeling we'd have all the ingredients by evening.

HALKARA

There are anima trees relatively close to the house, aren't there?

AZUSA

Yeah. They don't usually grow in the highlands, though, since it gets pretty warm in the summer.

HALKARA

The anima tree is somewhat common in the elf lands, though. Oh…

AZUSA

Hmm? What's wrong?

HALKARA

My chest caught on a tree branch.

AZUSA

Is this spite? Are you doing that to spite me?

HALKARA

Madam Teacher, what really matters is how they're shaped.

AZUSA

What's that supposed to mean? Those are the words of someone who's already winning.

HALKARA

There aren't many advantages to having a large chest… And more importantly, the anima tree is poisonous, so please be careful. Elves tend to avoid it.

AZUSA

More hallucinogens…? I wouldn't be surprised, after the last two…

HALKARA

Not that sort of poison. But if you keep touching it, your hand will break out in a rash. It's much safer to use gloves when harvesting them.

AZUSA

…You actually sound like an elf pharmacist today.

HALKARA

I don't just sound like one, I *am* one. You have a sharp tongue, Madam Teacher!

AZUSA

But if it's the type of poison that causes rashes, then we shouldn't need to worry. I was concerned it might turn people into animals or something, like the name says.

HALKARA

Oh, absolutely not. We'll find the leaves, then have Miss Beelzebub make curreh for dinner tonight!

AZUSA

You're really excited about this, huh?

HALKARA

That's because I've been drinking Nature's Power Juice, a special concoction I made that melts leftover alcohol in the body.

AZUSA

There you go making more weird drinks… But I've never heard of that one before.

HALKARA

I'm currently testing it out. I'm hoping to market it as long as there are no side effects. I just know there will be high demand for such a product!

AZUSA

Side effects… I don't like the sound of that…

HALKARA

You worry too much, Madam Teacher! It contains no deadly poisons or anything like that. One might get a little excited, but I've kept it within legal bounds. So it's all right! It's definitely fine!

AZUSA

When you tell me something is "definitely fine," that's a big red flag…

✽ ✽ ✽

Rustling grass.

HALKARA
Oh! That's an anima tree. We found one!
AZUSA
Its branches are growing out the sides, like horns. It stands out a lot more than I expected.
HALKARA
Once we get these, it'll be mission complete! See, Madam Teacher? Not a problem, *graaah*! The only thing left to do is go home, *graaah*!

Halkara goes into animal mode.

AZUSA
…Halkara, did you just roar?
HALKARA
Oh… My thoughts are getting cloudy… It's so very difficult to walk on two feet, *graaah*… Is this a side effect of Nature's Power Juice, *graaah*?!
AZUSA
Look at you! You're being overcome by some mysterious power! Hey! Don't go crawling around on all fours! It's unladylike!
HALKARA
Graaah, graaah! I'm the monster, Elfizard! *Graaah*…
AZUSA
And now you're babbling! I have a Cure Poison spell, so wait there!
HALKARA
The drink has already permeated my entire body, *graaah*. It's too late for a cure, *graaah*.
AZUSA
Why are you acting so calm?!

HALKARA
Because Elfizard the Monster is smart, *graaah*!
AZUSA
This is bad… If she goes totally wild and strays too far into the forest, she'll get hurt… I guess I have no choice but to take care of her myself.
HALKARA
Food, food, food… Mice, rabbits, foxes…
AZUSA
Oh no! Now all she can think about is hunting!
HALKARA
Wolves, dragons, golems…
AZUSA
Okay, there's no way you can hunt those. And you can't eat a golem! C'mon, Halkara. Come here. C'mere! I'm not gonna hurt you, I mean it. C'mere! Pspsps.
HALKARA
My name is Elfizard the Monster! *Graaah!*
AZUSA
I'm getting kind of annoyed by this fixation on your fictional identity… Uh, c'mon, Elfizard! C'mere! Come with me and I'll feed you chicken and pork and beef!
HALKARA
Elfizard the Monster prefers the vegetarian lifestyle.
AZUSA
So that part of you is still an elf, huh…? Well, then stop talking about wild mice and rabbits! You're getting your own lore mixed up!
HALKARA
But this human looks the tastiest! *Graaah!*

* * *

Halkara leaps at Azusa.

AZUSA
Whoa, whoa! Keep control of yourself! You leaped at me, and I fell on my butt…

HALKARA
Elfizard the Monster is an animal, so I establish my dominance by pouncing on others, *graaah*!

AZUSA
I was hoping that was a metaphor, but you're actually trying to get on top of me…

HALKARA
When the other is female, Elfizard the Monster establishes dominance by showing off how big my breasts are, *graaah*!

AZUSA
Gah! Stop pushing those against me! This is just spite, and I know it! And there's no way these things should be so bouncy!

HALKARA
Elfizard the Monster will now attempt to rub her scent on the other! This is called marking, *graaah*!

AZUSA
Stop it! That tickles! Don't lick my face! Maybe if you were a cat or a dog—but you're Halkara! An elf girl!

HALKARA
You smell so good, Madam Teacher… Oh, my head… Something else is trying to push Elfizard the Monster out of me, *woof*.

AZUSA
No, you're on the right track! Please win, Halkara! And stop licking me!

HALKARA

I'm Elfizard, *woof!*

AZUSA

You stopped roaring and started barking! Your own backstory is getting all mixed up!

HALKARA

Graaah, graaah! I'm going to lick you more! *Graaah!*

AZUSA

Ah! Ah-ha-ha-ha! Stop! My neck's ticklish! That's against the rules!

HALKARA

You're so much cuter than normal today, Madam Teacher. You're… You know. How do I say it. Brimming? …*Graaah.*

AZUSA

Brimming with what?! And you're basically back to normal! You're Halkara! You're not a monster!

HALKARA

Halkara…? I feel as though I've heard that useless elf's name somewhere before…

AZUSA

Why the self-deprecation? This sure is taking a while… Go cool off and change back— Oh, I know!

HALKARA

Graaah, graaah, graaah!

AZUSA

I'll cool you off with my ice magic!

Sound of a spell being cast.

AZUSA

Here, nice and cold! Now remember who you are!

HALKARA

Eep! That's freezing! Ooh… Ah, ah, ah-*choo*! Ooh… I'm going to get sick.

AZUSA
Finally, you're talking like Halkara again!
HALKARA
………Oh, I feel like I just woke up from an odd dream…
AZUSA
Halkara, is that you?! Are you back to normal?
HALKARA
Yes, Madam Teacher. I'm Halkara. Did something happen?
AZUSA
I'll tell you everything later. First, could you get off me?
HALKARA
Um… Ahhhhhhh! I'm sorry! I'm so sorry! What have I…? Please forgive me! I'll do anything!
AZUSA
Then could you get the anima leaves for us…?

AZUSA – NARRATION
And so, though I went through a lot of trouble to do it, I eventually got the spices needed to make curreh. All that was left was for me to make the dish with Beelzebub. I had been the one to bring it up in the first place, after all.

SCENE 7

Azusa and Beelzebub stand in the kitchen.

BEELZEBUB
Oh-ho. At last, we have all the spices. The door to curreh shall finally open!

AZUSA
Why are you making such a big deal out of this…?
BEELZEBUB
Because I have work tomorrow. I'm making the most of my remaining time off.
AZUSA
That's a little too real for me.
BEELZEBUB
Now we shall begin preparing the curreh. First, cut the onions, carrots, other vegetables, and the chicken into bite-size chunks. We shall be making chicken curreh this time.
AZUSA
Just like curry. I'll help cut.
BEELZEBUB
And I have precut ingredients over here.
AZUSA
You cut them already?!
BEELZEBUB
We put these into a big pot, then cook them thoroughly for about thirty minutes on low heat. The trick is to keep watch until the onions get soft and take on a caramel color.
AZUSA
I'll do that part, then.
BEELZEBUB
And here are the ingredients already cooked for thirty minutes.
AZUSA
You made them already?!
BEELZEBUB
This work can all be done without the spices, so I went ahead and did it.
AZUSA
Wait, hold on! You're not gonna turn around and

tell me you've already finished cooking the whole thing, are you…? I'm going to be mad if you're putting all my spices to waste.

BEELZEBUB

N-no, of course not… Once the ingredients are well cooked, add water to the pot, then bring it all to a boil. Make sure to stir it every once in a while so nothing sticks to the bottom of the pot.

AZUSA

I can do that. But this really is just curry…

BEELZEBUB

Mix it veeery well. We demons have a saying about this part of the curreh-making process: The more you stir, the more the color changes!

AZUSA

I feel like I've heard that somewhere before, like in a candy commercial… *Mix, mix, mix. Mix, mix, mix.* If you think of this as a stew, I guess it isn't all that weird that it exists here, too. Oh, the pot's getting hotter.

BEELZEBUB

See? See? Once we add everything to the pot, it will turn into curreh in an instant.

AZUSA

I bet you need to add some kind of secret curreh powder. Otherwise, it won't be like what was in the bread we had this morning.

BEELZEBUB

Oh-ho-ho. We'll be adding this next: Ultimate Curreh Roux!

AZUSA

That looks like roux I used to buy at the store.

BEELZEBUB

Most demon families keep Ultimate Curreh Roux at home. One can easily achieve restaurant-quality food using this.

AZUSA

If it was so easy, then you shouldn't have sent me out to get those spices!

BEELZEBUB

Those spices will allow us to achieve an even richer flavor, which is why we add them as secret ingredients at the end. It will elevate our curreh to untold heights.

AZUSA

I don't really buy it... But okay. Well, I'm putting the roux in.

BEELZEBUB

Go on. Next, slowly melt the roux, and once its flavors have permeated all of the ingredients, it's finished. 'Tis very, very delicious!

AZUSA

No matter how I look at it, this is just curry...

BEELZEBUB

Next, mix in the ingredients you procured using my original ratio, and it's all done!

Ding **signaling completion.**

AZUSA

Ooh! It's looking good!

BEELZEBUB

Now let's get this into deep soup bowls and eat it with some bread. I wish to see Falfa's and Shalsha's delighted faces!

AZUSA
Yes. I can see we're all finished, but...
BEELZEBUB
Hmm?
AZUSA
There's one thing I want you to do, just in case.
BEELZEBUB
Like what? Do you want me to dance around it and chant to make it even tastier?
AZUSA
That won't change anything in the kitchen. I want you to taste-test it for me. To check for poison.
BEELZEBUB
How rude you are... You have seen for yourself what sorts of things are in the curreh...
AZUSA
But today was a disaster. Everyone got weird. What if the proportions are off? You won't suddenly freak out, too, will you? This could be dangerous. I can't risk my family eating any until it's been tested.
BEELZEBUB
Hmm... I suppose 'twould be best to give it a taste. I have heard that these ingredients were once used to create a love potion, but I believe that was just a myth. Nothing more.
AZUSA
Well, now you've jinxed it for sure!

Beelzebub takes a bite.

BEELZEBUB
Mmm. 'Tis indeed mellow, yet rich. This would put a professional to shame! Adding the spices really elevates the flavor.

AZUSA

It does *look* delicious. And it's been cooked well.

BEELZEBUB

See? Nothing's going to......... Ah, ohh... Ohh...!

AZUSA

Ack! Beelzebub! Are you okay?!

BEELZEBUB

I-i-it feels as though...my body is burning...

AZUSA

Was the curry too spicy?! C'mon, get a grip! Can you stand? If you can't, you can lean on me!

BEELZEBUB

A-A-A...Azusa...

AZUSA

What? Let's get you to a bed first, okay?

BEELZEBUB

You are...so pretty...

AZUSA

.........What?

BEELZEBUB

I feel my body alight with flame whenever I look at you... Will you help me cool this heat...?

Azusa pulls ice out of nowhere.

AZUSA

Okay, I thought this might happen, so I was prepared. I made some ice with magic.

BEELZEBUB

Pant, pant. Marry me and let Falfa and Shalsha be my real children...

AZUSA

Let's cool your forehead until you come back to your senses, okay? I see that even under the effects of the love potion, you're still after my daughters...

BEELZEBUB
S-so cold! Please do not treat me so roughly...!

Azusa pulls out even more ice from nowhere.

AZUSA
That didn't seem to be enough, so here's some more.
BEELZEBUB
That's so cold! So, so, so cold! Ah-*choo*! Oh dear, what have I done...? I mixed up the amounts of bab nuts and hacko herbs...
AZUSA
See? It's just one thing after another today. We'll start over.
BEELZEBUB
A-aye... My apologies...

AZUSA – NARRATION
Afterward, we remade the curreh and got it all on the table, ready for dinner.

SCENE 8

AZUSA
All right, here's dinner for today! Dip your bread in and eat up. There's a lot of tasty morsels inside!

Sounds of munching on bread.

LAIKA
Ohh! What an exciting flavor! I've never tasted

anything like this before. It feels as though my eyes have been opened!
AZUSA
I suppose it did turn out pretty spicy.
HALKARA
Ahhh! A strong drink would go wonderfully with this!
AZUSA
You think this would go well with booze…? Are you sure you're not just fishing for reasons to drink?

Sounds of munching on bread.

FALFA
This is super yummy! Thank you, Big Sis Beelzebub!
SHALSHA
Shalsha can eat as much bread as she likes. And the vegetables are well seasoned, so Shalsha doesn't mind them.
AZUSA
Oh yeah. Kids love curry.
BEELZEBUB
Not curry. Curreh.
AZUSA
Sure. Curreh. Okay.
FALFA
Falfa wants to eat this for a whole week!
BEELZEBUB
Is that so? Then I shall make it so just for you, Falfa.
AZUSA
Don't you have work tomorrow?

BEELZEBUB
Ah. I do... I must go to work...
AZUSA
Life is hard when you have a job, huh?
BEELZEBUB
Mmm, perhaps I shall come over on my next day off to make curreh...

AZUSA – NARRATION
Once Beelzebub had her curreh, she went back to the demon lands. All I had to do was wash the dishes.

HALKARA
Madam Teacher, may I have a moment?
AZUSA
Hmm? What's wrong, Halkara? Did you eat too much curreh?
HALKARA
I think there was a chunk of spices in my portion of the curreh... Ever since I ate it, my body feels very hot...

Halkara sidles up to Azusa.

AZUSA
...I have a bad feeling about this. Hold on a second—I'm going to make ice with my magic.
HALKARA
Madam Teacher, my body burns... I can't take it anymore!
AZUSA
No! You have to hold it in! This is *definitely* because of the spices!

HALKARA
Madam Teacher, could you please lick me?
AZUSA
No way! This is too much… Next time, we're making curry *without* any extra spices!

The End

This story is an edited version of the script of the first drama CD, contained in the special release edition of Volume 5.

This story takes place after "Halkara's Suspected Graduation" from Volume 2.

SCENE 1

Halkara is getting ready to open her new factory in Nascúte.

HALKARA
Phew. I've made so much progress on the Halkara Pharmaceuticals factory!
Now it's time for a lunch break. I suppose I'll have a bottle of my own company's energy drink, Nutri-Spirits!
…Or perhaps now is the time for *real* spirits?
Though I feel a little pathetic having booze so early in the day… This calls for careful consideration… I'm going to have a good hard think… Hmmmm. Hmmmmmm.

*　*　*

Time passes.

HALKARA
Yes! I've made my decision! I should have real spirits as a treat!
BEELZEBUB
What are you doing?
HALKARA
Gaaaaaaaah! M-M-M-M-Miss B-B-B-B-B-Beelzebub!
BEELZEBUB
What an overreaction… You've added too many *B*s to my name. And you made up your mind only seconds after saying you would consider the matter carefully.
HALKARA
What can I say? Adults are weak to alcohol!
BEELZEBUB
Speak for yourself. And what are you doing out here? This town is a bit far from the village near where you all live.
HALKARA
You say that, but the demon lands are even farther… And as it happens, I'm opening up a factory in Nascúte.
BEELZEBUB
Oh! At long last, Nutri-Spirits will be mass-produced! Praise be! I must buy as much as I can! No, perhaps I should purchase the entire factory with the ministry's budget!
HALKARA
Please do not buy my factory when I'm still in the process of building it!
BEELZEBUB
I was joking about buying the whole thing. Still, many felicitations to you.

HALKARA
Oh, that's right. Speaking of felicitations…
BEELZEBUB
Hmm? What happened?
HALKARA
Madam Teacher and the rest of the family held a celebration for me the other day. They'd misunderstood and thought I was leaving the house in the highlands, so they held a farewell party for me.
BEELZEBUB
…Azusa does seem the sort to jump the gun.
HALKARA
And I thought perhaps we could celebrate Madam Teacher in return!
BEELZEBUB
Mmm, an admirable mindset. She would be delighted.
HALKARA
You must know of unique demon dishes, like how you made curreh for us last time. Would you…happen to know of anything suitable for a celebration?
BEELZEBUB
Let's see. Rather than a regular party, I believe Azusa would have more fun if we served her a dish she is unfamiliar with. Hmm, hmm.

Time passes.

BEELZEBUB
I've got it. I know of a dish just as unique to demon culture as curreh!
HALKARA
Please, tell me!
BEELZEBUB
The name of this dish comes from the word *lament*.

HALKARA
That sounds inauspicious...
BEELZEBUB
'Tis a noodle dish called ra-ment. We call it so because 'tis so scrumptious, one cannot help but cry.
HALKARA
Ra-ment? The name alone sounds delicious!
BEELZEBUB
But we need several different ingredients to make good ra-ment broth. At the very least, we will require chicken bones, pork bones, and dried sardines.
HALKARA
That's fine. I'm certain Miss Laika, Falfa, and Shalsha will help!

BEELZEBUB – NARRATION
And so Halkara and I ventured to the house in the highlands and met with Laika the dragon and the two girls who are essentially my daughters, Falfa and Shalsha. Then we held a meeting on how we would procure the necessary ingredients.

SCENE 2

House in the highlands – dining room.

BEELZEBUB
And so we will need chicken bones, pork bones, and dried sardines. The quality of these ingredients will determine the quality of the ra-ment. Would you happen to know of any good places where

we can find them? Danger is no obstacle—I shall accompany you, so please do not be shy.

HALKARA

I know of a forest said to be home to an elusive bird whose bones make great stock.

BEELZEBUB

Ah yes. You know your forests, as an elf should. Then I shall accompany you.

Azusa suddenly enters from behind Beelzebub.

AZUSA

Beelzebub? What are you talking about with everyone else?

BEELZEBUB

I-it has nothing to do with you! I am preparing documents for a very important demon meeting!

AZUSA

...Are you sure you can show those to Laika and Halkara? You're not breaking any rules as minister? Isn't that a breach of confidentiality?

BEELZEBUB

'Tis not that sort of document. I can show others without repercussions.

AZUSA

So it's not a problem if you show me, then. C'mon, let's see them!

BEELZEBUB

You are the one person who cannot see! I am very, very, very serious!

AZUSA

This just makes me more suspicious... You're not thinking of a foolproof way to defeat me or anything, are you?

LAIKA

It is nothing like that, Lady Azusa! It is perfectly safe and reasonable! I swear on my red-dragon horns!

AZUSA

Well, if you say so…

FALFA

Don't worry about it, Mommy. Worrying is like going through the bad thing before it happens!

SHALSHA

Indeed. To be precise, it is a trivial matter. Like the hair on a worm.

AZUSA

If I worry, I suffer twice? I'm not sure if that phrase fits the situation, Falfa… And do worms even have hair…?

FALFA

It's really nice outside, Mommy! You should go chase grasshoppers! I bet there are lots of ladybugs, too! You should take a walk!

AZUSA

I'm not *that* interested in bugs. In fact, I'd rather not see *any*.

SHALSHA

Walking helps one organize one's thoughts, and it becomes easier to reach the truth. A certain philosopher arrived at the main thesis of his work while on a walk. You should try it, Mom. It will bring you good health and brighten all our lives.

AZUSA

You're pushing for a walk so hard that I'm starting to think you're a shill for the walking industry…

LAIKA
Lady Azusa, do get some fresh air! I will finish the cleaning, so you have no need to worry.
AZUSA
What's up with all of you...? Oh well, I guess there's no harm in it. I'll go for a walk.

Azusa leaves.

BEELZEBUB
...Phew. We were not found out. Now, the pork bone. Are there any places known for their pigs?
FALFA
Oh! Falfa and Shalsha know!
SHALSHA
There is a forest said to be home to delectable pigs.
BEELZEBUB
Aw, you're both so smart. Such good children! So cute! So adorable! Very well, you shall both come with me!

Azusa enters again.

AZUSA
Beelzebub, are you going somewhere with my kids? Don't take them anywhere too dangerous.
BEELZEBUB
Bah! I know! In fact, I will treat them with more respect than you do! I shall spoil them rotten!
AZUSA
I don't like the sound of that, either.
FALFA
Mommy, Falfa is going to be good.

SHALSHA

Shalsha will listen to what Miss Beelzebub says. Shalsha will be disciplined.

BEELZEBUB

Ahhh, they're so cute! I wish I could adopt them! I want to leave all my assets to them!

AZUSA

No. Absolutely not. You cannot adopt children without their parents' consent.

BEELZEBUB

I jest, of course. Now go for your walk. Relax at a fancy café or something. I cannot put my documents together like this.

AZUSA

I don't think there are any fancy cafés like that around here.

BEELZEBUB

I don't care! Get out! If you don't like it, I shall apologize to you properly later. But for now, leave!

AZUSA

Fine, fine. I was just preparing some medicine to bring to the village on my walk. I'll be out of here soon.

Azusa leaves again.

LAIKA

That was close.

BEELZEBUB

But she's yet to find us out, so we are safe. Lastly, we need dried sardines—a product of the sea. Would any of you happen to have knowledge of the ocean?

LAIKA

I'll do it! I will quickly become an expert on dried sardines, then find a location that provides the absolute best! I shall obtain dried sardines that will leave Lady Azusa speechless!

BEELZEBUB

You are much too enthusiastic for this...

LAIKA

It is part of my training! A chance to grow! And...I want Lady Azusa to eat the best ra-ment in the entire world... Nothing would make me happier than to see her beaming with delight...

BEELZEBUB

Well, so long as you're motivated, I suppose. Now then, Halkara will get the bird, Falfa and Shalsha will fetch the pig, and Laika will find the sardines. I shall accompany all of you, so never fear.

Azusa enters again.

AZUSA

Are you planning on going somewhere? Then you should include me, too!

BEELZEBUB

No! Please, stop talking to us, or it will all be for nothing! Go on your walk! Or are you engaging in walking fraud?!

AZUSA

Beelzebub, your vibes are way off today. You're like one of those demons who humans used to fear.

BEELZEBUB

I doubt the demons of old merely had "bad vibes" like some off-putting coworker! And anyway, in the long term, you will benefit from what we are doing, so worry not.

LAIKA
Miss Beelzebub, you are getting very close to disclosing the information. Be careful.

FALFA
Mommy, it is well-known that if someone takes a walk on this day, they will be especially lucky. That goes double if you are a witch! They say you'll be happy for the rest of your life!

AZUSA
It sounds like not a lot of people can benefit...

SHALSHA
When you achieve a satisfying sense of exertion from your walk, your health will improve, as will your sleep quality. Walks solve all problems. Walks can bring peace to the universe.

AZUSA
Are you sure you're not starting a new religion...? I feel like things are only getting more complicated here, so I'm definitely, definitely off on my walk now!

BEELZEBUB
That sounded like a bluff, so I do not know if I should trust her.

BEELZEBUB – NARRATION
First, Halkara and I ventured out in search of a chicken.

SCENE 3

Beelzebub and Halkara go to the forest and look for a chicken.

HALKARA
We're here! This is the forest! Ooh, I'm going to hurl...
BEELZEBUB
We've only just arrived. Are you out of energy already...?
HALKARA
I drank too much yesterday. It was so strange. I meant to have only one glass, but I ended up having seven.
BEELZEBUB
What is strange is your lack of self-restraint.
HALKARA
We will be searching for a bird called the kobe chicken.
BEELZEBUB
...For some reason, I am picturing a cow instead of a chicken.
HALKARA
Incidentally, this forest is called the Might-Have-Been-Lost Woods, and people fear it.
BEELZEBUB
But that name implies no one was actually lost.
HALKARA
According to legend, if you close your eyes and spin around while saying *"belfant renre tontola cydrovish"* five times without getting tongue-tied, then you'll be cursed.

BEELZEBUB
Enacting the curse sounds much too difficult! No one will be cursed so!

HALKARA
But it is true that people call it the Might-Have-Been-Lost Woods. There was once an elf marathon held here, and thirty percent of the participants got lost and ultimately dropped out.

BEELZEBUB
All those who oversaw the marathon should be fired. And what is so special about this kobe chicken?

HALKARA
The kobe chicken caws in a very unique way. Please tell me if you hear an unusual cry.

BEELZEBUB
All right. I will be very attentive. Shall we?

Rustling grass.

BEELZEBUB
Oh!

HALKARA
What is it?

BEELZEBUB
I heard a rather gross-sounding cry. It went, "*doofoofoo, doofoofoo.*" Could that be our chicken?

HALKARA
Oh, that's the groce bird. It's a different species.

BEELZEBUB
It was, indeed, a gross cry, but what an awful name...

HALKARA
It's a favorite of grocers.

BEELZEBUB
Oh, is *that* where the name comes from?!

Rustling grass.

BEELZEBUB
Oh! I hear another strange cry!
HALKARA
What did it sound like?
BEELZEBUB
It went, "*Hyaha! Hyaha!*" Could that be it?
HALKARA
Oh, that's the third-rate unimportant bird.
BEELZEBUB
Was the one who was naming these creatures in a bad mood?!
HALKARA
Its flavor is third-rate and therefore not suitable for cooking.
BEELZEBUB
This forest is full of strange birds… Hmm?! That was the most unique sound I've heard thus far!
HALKARA
What did it sound like?
BEELZEBUB
As though it were calling, "*Big bro! Big bro!*"
HALKARA
Oh, that's the little sister bird.
BEELZEBUB
Why not make it the little brother bird?! Why must it be a sister?!
HALKARA
It gained its name because men who want little sisters are willing to pay a high price for them.

BEELZEBUB

It sounds like those men have crossed a line!

HALKARA

I hear they have the birds wake them up by calling, "*Big bro!*" each morning.

BEELZEBUB

I do not wish to hear its uses! I want nothing to do with any of it!

The sound of a cow?

BEELZEBUB

There are cows in these woods?

HALKARA

That's it! That is the cry of the kobe chicken!

BEELZEBUB

You should have told me it sounded like a cow to begin with!

HALKARA

I heard it! The Yonezawa Omi chicken is just ahead!

BEELZEBUB

That's a totally different name! You were calling it the kobe chicken mere moments earlier! What is the Yonezawa Omi chicken?! 'Tis an entirely different thing!

HALKARA

It's fine. They're both very high-quality birds. We'll just say it's a brand-name chicken, and no one will be able to tell the difference.

BEELZEBUB

No need to get excited... Oh, but the mooing is growing louder. We must be close!

* * *

The Yonezawa Omi chicken cries.

HALKARA
On the count of three, we leap at the chicken!
BEELZEBUB
I don't think that will be necessary. It's coming straight for you.
HALKARA
What? Ahhh! Something's coming! It's pecking me! It's pecking me! Oh yes! I caught it! It's mine!
BEELZEBUB
Actually, 'tis still pecking at you…but you did successfully capture it. Well done!
HALKARA
Ow! Ouch! Its beak is sharp!
BEELZEBUB
What a relentless attack…
HALKARA
Oh…… Oh no……
BEELZEBUB
What? What happened?!
HALKARA
Miss Beelzebub? I have some bad news.
BEELZEBUB
What? Out with it…
HALKARA
This is a different type of brand-name chicken, called the Saga chicken.
BEELZEBUB
I do not care anymore!

* * *

BEELZEBUB - NARRATION
Next, Falfa, Shalsha, and I went to find a pig. Good pork bone is crucial in ra-ment... And even if we do not find it, nothing makes me happier than the thought of traveling with the girls.

SCENE 4

Beelzebub, Falfa, and Shalsha venture into the woods in search of a pig.

FALFA
Yes! This has to be the place. We're here, we're here!
SHALSHA
A land of deep mountain valleys. The perfect place for a sage to seclude herself.
BEELZEBUB
This place is indeed remote. Do not stray. Hold on to my hands.
FALFA
Okay, Miss Beelzebub.
SHALSHA
Thank you, Miss Beelzebub.
BEELZEBUB
Doofoofoo... You may call me Mother, if you like. I do not mind a bit. I shall buy you anything you like. *Doofoofoo...*
SHALSHA
Miss Beelzebub, you're laughing like the groce bird.

BEELZEBUB

That bird is more well-known than I thought...

FALFA

There's a legend about this forest. It says there are tanuki that can use magic and turn into people!

SHALSHA

There are folk tales of tanuki and foxes tricking people all across the land. They are especially prominent in this area.

BEELZEBUB

Well, no great demon such as myself could ever be duped by such creatures. But do be careful, you two.

FALFA

Oh wow! Cool!

SHALSHA

This is astounding.

BEELZEBUB

What did you find?

SHALSHA

Shalsha did not know there were houses made of candy and cookies in the forest.

BEELZEBUB

This is most certainly a tanuki's trick!

FALFA

Wow! Let's go, let's go! Falfa's going to eat all the cookies she wants! There are macarons, too! And chocolate!

SHALSHA

Sometimes, one must go...even knowing they are being duped.

BEELZEBUB

No! Stay put, you two. That's dangerous!

FALFA

Huh? Wait, look at the candy...

SHALSHA

...It's all made of fallen leaves and earth; it only looks like cookies and pastries from far away...

BEELZEBUB

What an odd way to dupe people! Don't tanuki use magic to disguise things?! This is just a testament to hard work!

FALFA

What's it like inside? Let's go! Falfa's so excited!

SHALSHA

An ancient scholar once said that there is no drug more dangerous than curiosity.

BEELZEBUB

If you can recall such advice, then do not go inside!

The door opens.

BEELZEBUB

Mmm, 'tis empty, though it is more like a regular house than I expected.

FALFA

Oh, there's a notice on the wall.

SHALSHA

It says *Five reasons why tanuki are better than foxes*.

BEELZEBUB

Why are the tanuki self-advertising?! Do they have no intention of tricking us?

FALFA

Hmm. This must be a tanuki exhibition space. Shalsha would like this kind of thing, I think.

SHALSHA

It is terribly fascinating. There is a flag here that says *Retake the government from the foxes!*

BEELZEBUB

What government?! Are they residents of the same country?!

FALFA

This one says *Let's trick the foxes into giving us more votes!*

BEELZEBUB

I do not recommend that as a political slogan.

FALFA

Oh! There's a place over there for getting to know tanuki!

BEELZEBUB

Falfa, do not run so far ahead!

Falfa meets a pack of tanuki.

FALFA

Wow! There's so many tanuki! But...they're a lot dirtier than the ones in my picture books...

BEELZEBUB

'Tis because the tanuki in the books are made to look cute!

FALFA

Oh, I see. These tanuki aren't earning enough money despite all their hard work. They're being exploited by the capitalist tanuki...

BEELZEBUB

'Tis a difficult world! Especially for tanuki!

FALFA

That tanuki has been rubbing its hands like it's scheming this whole time!

BEELZEBUB

That's not a tanuki; that's a raccoon.

SHALSHA

This exhibit details the combined history of tanuki and raccoons.

BEELZEBUB

These animals seem quite advanced.

SHALSHA

It appears fifty-one percent are in favor of merging the two groups, with forty-nine percent opposed.

BEELZEBUB

What a narrow margin!

SHALSHA

This establishment details the history of the tanuki's hardships, frustrations, and anger without abbreviation. It has been terribly educational.

FALFA

Wooow, the tanuki are so soft and fluffy! Falfa is so happy!

SHALSHA

Sis, you forget our original objective. We are here to find a pig…to pet the fuzzy tanuki.

BEELZEBUB

You are both losing out to your momentary desires… But I suppose 'tis fine. Seeing your delighted faces gives me the greatest joy in life.

FALFA

Oh! The tanuki brought us cookies!

SHALSHA

The one on the right tastes like a delicious cookie, but it is actually grass. The one on the left is an actual cookie, but it tastes terrible, like grass.

BEELZEBUB

A difficult decision, indeed!

FALFA

Then Falfa will pick the grass that tastes like tasty cookies!

SHALSHA

Shalsha will do the same.

BEELZEBUB

You both went straight for the grass!

The sound of crunching cookies.

FALFA

Wooow! This is the tastiest cookie Falfa's ever eaten! Falfa doesn't even care if it's grass!

SHALSHA

If the brain interprets it as tasty, then that is the truth. One could even say the whole world is an illusion shown to us by the brain.

BEELZEBUB

Well, then I suppose I may as well try the real cookie.

The sound of crunching cookies.

BEELZEBUB

…Ugh! As expected of a cookie made by tanuki! They are so dry and brittle!

FALFA

Oh, the tanuki say they'll take us to the best pig if we make their wishes come true.

BEELZEBUB

Oh-ho. Though I suppose it will be troublesome if their wish ends up taking us a long time…

SHALSHA

They say, "Our shoulders are stiff. We want massages."

BEELZEBUB
Consider it done!

BEELZEBUB - NARRATION
We massaged the tanuki's shoulders and safely got our rare pig. This would net us our pork bone. Soon, we would have all our ingredients. Finally, Laika and I made for the ocean to get the dried sardines. We chartered a fishing boat to get out onto the water.

SCENE 5

Laika and Beelzebub set sail on rough seas.
The sound of whipping wind.

LAIKA
It's quite rough out here. I did not think it would be storming out in the middle of the ocean.
BEELZEBUB
Indeed. We run the risk of capsizing on such a small fishing boat.
LAIKA
We do. I'm certain I'd get seasick if we were on the boat.
BEELZEBUB
Thankfully, that is not a problem, since I am hoisting you up as I float.

* * *

Laika exhales.

LAIKA
Sigh. Sorry to trouble you. I can't fly in my human form.

BEELZEBUB
Worry not. I am a high-ranking demon. Carrying you alone is nothing... And you cannot fish in your dragon form anyway.

LAIKA
Oh, the captain is crying. He says, "We might capsize. Please let me turn back to port."

BEELZEBUB
If we capsize, then Laika can turn into a dragon and save you. Worry not.

LAIKA
He says, "I cannot work with a capsized boat." And something about a fisherman's boat being his life.

BEELZEBUB
Then I shall buy you a new one with my ministry's budget. Matters relating to agriculture, forestry, and fisheries should not be a problem.

LAIKA
I am not sure if that is an appropriate use of public funds...

BEELZEBUB
'Tis fine. Much more aboveboard than tanuki and fox politics.

LAIKA
What? Tanuki and foxes are involved in politics? That is news to me...

BEELZEBUB
...Do not concern yourself with the details.

LAIKA
Oh, the captain is delighted to hear he might get a new boat. He is now expressing his wish that this old rotten junk heap would just sink already.
BEELZEBUB
Was he not saying his boat was his life mere moments ago?! Anyway, this is the right spot for the sardines, yes? I do not know much of the ocean.
LAIKA
It seems we need only collect the fish called conceit sardines located in this area.
BEELZEBUB
Conceit sardines? What color are they? What sort of unique characteristics do they have?
LAIKA
Apparently, they get very carried away, insisting that they are incredibly strong and powerful.
BEELZEBUB
You are supposed to tell me what they *look* like… There must be humble conceit sardines…

Laika notices a noise from below.

LAIKA
Oh, the captain has begun lifting the net. Let's go down and check the catch!
BEELZEBUB
Aye! We shall help pull up the net as well. Heave ho!
LAIKA
Heave ho! Heave ho! Heave ho! Heave ho! Heave ho! Heave ho!
BEELZEBUB
You're quite serious about this…

LAIKA

We are doing this so that we may feed Lady Azusa the very best ra-ment! Please wait just a little longer, Lady Azusa!

BEELZEBUB

How admirable... I feel water in my eyes... Is it raining?

Ah, are these little ones the conceit sardines?

LAIKA

No, those are obsequor sardines. Look at their faces. They practically scream, *I am nothing but a weakling. I can't accomplish anything.*

BEELZEBUB

'Tis only your own bias. I am certain there are those among them who think, *One day I shall rule over all of sardine-kind. Watch out.*

LAIKA

Either way, they do not taste as good as conceit sardines, so please throw them back into the water.

BEELZEBUB

Yes. We must conserve our natural resources and release everything we will not use for food! Grow big and strong in the sea! Abandon your obsequiousness...! Oh, this sardine looks different from the other ones.

LAIKA

Yes! That is a conceit sardine! It's not very big, but it's showing off with incredible jumps there. Please put it in the basket there.

BEELZEBUB

Yes. That marks our first catch. Oh, this one here is quite large.

LAIKA

That is a large bonito. It sells for a rather high price, but it is not our sardine, so please put it back in the water.

BEELZEBUB

Catch and release! Ah, now we have a crab.

LAIKA

That is a red king crab—a prized delicacy in some regions, but it is not a sardine, so please put it back in the water.

BEELZEBUB

Catch and release! Oh? Another fish.

LAIKA

That is a golden eye snapper. Another top-grade fish, but it is not our sardine, so please put it back in the water.

BEELZEBUB

Catch and release! Ooh... This next fish is massive! The captain looks delighted, too.

LAIKA

This is...the biggest a bluefin tuna can get. Well, it is not a sardine, so please put it back in the water.

BEELZEBUB

Catch and release! We don't need these! There are plenty, but we need none of them!

LAIKA

Oh, there are plenty of conceit sardines over here! Let's gather them up. Captain? Why are you crying? What? You wanted me to keep the tuna and the crab? But we only have need of the sardines.

BEELZEBUB

By the way, Laika. A thought.

LAIKA

Yes?

BEELZEBUB

To make dried sardines, we will ultimately need to...well, dry the sardines, no? They must sell high-quality dried sardines somewhere.

LAIKA

…Oh. You may be right. I am sorry. Once I concentrate on one thing, it is very hard for me to think about other things… I was too fixated on the sardines themselves.

BEELZEBUB

Ah, 'tis all right. Then let us return to port and find some dried sardines.

LAIKA

Is something the matter, Captain? Oh yes. We returned all the tuna back to the water. Why are you crying so hard? Did something bad happen? It's all right! Regret will only lead to further growth! Please do not give up! Keep going! I am here to support you!

BEELZEBUB

That only made him cry even harder. I suppose 'tis true that one's tears fall more freely as one gets older.

BEELZEBUB – NARRATION

We purchased very nice dried sardines at the harbor. I knew where to get noodles as well, which meant all our ingredients were accounted for. Now it was time to make ra-ment!

SCENE 6

In the dining room of the house in the highlands again.

AZUSA

I'm home! I'm finally back from the walk you told me to go on. To be honest, nothing interesting happened. It was so peaceful! I yawned at least five times! But better that than trouble, right? …Hmm? You're all gathered together again. What's going on? I see you finished up with the factory early today, Halkara. And Beelzebub's here, too.

HALKARA

Madam Teacher, do you remember the other day when you thought I was leaving the house in the highlands and threw a party for me?

AZUSA

Oh yeah… I mean, you were looking at so much property, I honestly thought you were ready to go solo… But it turned out you were just looking for land for your factory.

HALKARA

Still, you threw me a party, so we thought it'd be nice to return the favor!

FALFA

Falfa and Shalsha helped find ingredients, too!

SHALSHA

We even ate grass to find you good pork.

AZUSA

What? Where did you two go that you wound up starving?

FALFA

But the grass tasted like really yummy cookies!

SHALSHA

I want the tanuki to dupe me again.

AZUSA

It tasted like cookies? Tanuki? ...Sorry, what you're saying is so fantastical that even a three-hundred-year-old like me can't understand.

LAIKA

We decided to treat you to a unique demon dish, Lady Azusa. I joined in as well, since I am thankful for you every day.

BEELZEBUB

And I, the demon of the group, was in charge of cooking!

AZUSA

Aww, guys, thank you... I've never had anyone throw me a surprise party. I'm so happy! I had a lot of surprise *work* when I was a corporate slave... And when I thought I was finally caught up, I'd have even more work waiting for me...

LAIKA

Lady Azusa? What is wrong?

AZUSA

Sorry, it's nothing. Just a little painful memory from the past. All right, pass me the demon grub!

BEELZEBUB

I shall! This is our demon dish, ra-ment! It gets quite hot if you eat it with a metal fork, so be sure to use a wooden one!

AZUSA

Wow, this is really a typical bowl of ramen! I didn't think they'd have ramen here, too... They really have everything...

BEELZEBUB

'Tis not ramen! 'Tis ra-ment! You pronounce it wrong!

AZUSA
Why are you picky about what it's called...? In my eyes, this is ramen.
BEELZEBUB
You pronounced my curreh sloppily as "curry" last time, no? I wish you would remember the proper names for these dishes. Wouldn't you be furious if someone called you Bazusa?
AZUSA
If this world is going to have the same kinds of food, I wish they'd use the same names. It's such a hassle...
BEELZEBUB
Your noodles will not be as good if you do not eat them quickly. Hurry up and dig in.
AZUSA
Guess you're right. Fine. Time for some good old-fashioned ramen...t.

Azusa drinks some of the broth.

AZUSA
Ooh! I can taste chicken and pork bone and dried sardines.

What a relief—there are no preservatives! Because it's got a mix of ingredients, it's missing the punch, but the flavors are layered. I could see myself coming back for more again and again!

I can clearly taste the dried sardines, but I don't detect their usual bitterness. And though the pork bone isn't gamey at all, you've really drawn out a powerful umami from it! The chicken bones have been boiled thoroughly, too. But the bones aren't the only thing, are they? By boiling the feet and the skin, too, you've brought out that gentle sweetness and mellow richness, like a mother's cooking, that can only come from chicken! What's more, no one flavor overpowers the others. You've really achieved the golden ratio to make this a perfect trinity!

FALFA

Falfa's never seen Mommy talk so much about food!

SHALSHA

It seems she has a lot to say about this dish.

AZUSA

And these thin noodles suit the broth perfectly! I can even taste the flavor of the wheat! This is freshly made, isn't it?! The wheat's natural sweetness sits nicely in the background and doesn't interfere with the flavor of the broth!

FALFA

Mommy has so much to say!

SHALSHA

Incredible. She's like a poet.

AZUSA

Actually, I don't know all that much about ramen. There's just something about it that makes me want to talk. Ah… Those late-night ramen joints took such good care of me when I was a corporate slave…

BEELZEBUB

Yes, yes! Isn't it good? That is the most traditional kind of ra-ment one can get, but it is a very difficult dish to master!

LAIKA

Apologies, Lady Azusa. What should I do with the vegetables, the oil, and the garlic?

AZUSA

What are you talking about? I'm not sure what you want, but go ahead and do as you like, Laika.

LAIKA

Understood!

FALFA

Mommy? Pick a number from one to ten!

SHALSHA

This is the moment we test you, Mom.

AZUSA

What are you asking me now? Is this a personality test? Or maybe you're hoping to win with a three. Well then, I'll pick ten.

FALFA

Okay! Then we'll put in a lot!

SHALSHA

You are incredible, Mom. We respect you. You are a real trooper.

AZUSA

Well, that was easy. I've earned their respect simply by picking the number ten… By the way, Beelzebub. I had no idea you could make such high-quality ramen…t.

BEELZEBUB

To tell you the truth, one of my subordinates has the skills of a professional chef. Her name is Vania. She was helping up until a moment ago.

AZUSA

She came all the way out here for this…? I guess I'll have to thank her.

BEELZEBUB

She left. She has work, or so she says.

AZUSA

You really just brought her over to cook…? Now I feel bad…

BEELZEBUB

Well, you shall meet her when the time comes. 'Tis the way of things. And…'tis not an exaggeration to say that ra-ment is like life itself.

AZUSA
I *do* think that's an exaggeration, but I get what you're saying.

Azusa eats the ra-ment.

AZUSA
It's been ages since I had ramen. That was fantastic.
BEELZEBUB
Ra-ment.
AZUSA
...This ra-ment was so good! Thank you!
HALKARA
Miss Laika! She finished the first bowl!
AZUSA
What? What do you mean, first bowl?
HALKARA
For your celebration, we prepared several different types of ra-ment.
AZUSA
What?! I'm getting two bowls?!
LAIKA
Another bowl of ra-ment coming up! Here you go, Lady Azusa!
AZUSA
Whoooaaa! Look at all the vegetables heaped on top, and how stiff these thick noodles are... Back in Japan, we called overloaded ramen like this Yujiro-style ramen.
BEELZEBUB
No, not Yujiro-style. This is Jiro-style. 'Tis another classic kind of ra-ment. There are some demons who are so obsessed with Jiro-style ra-ment that they have built shrines to it.

AZUSA
They even worship it…
LAIKA
Apparently, a staple of Jiro-style ra-ment is to ask how much vegetable and oil to put in, as well as whether or not you wish to add garlic.
AZUSA
So that's what that question was about!
LAIKA
When I asked you previously, you told me to do as I like, so I added a lot of each to make it to the dragon standard.
AZUSA
Why did you make it to the dragon standard?! Make it to the seventeen-year-old human girl standard! But isn't it a little weird to serve this second…? This is the kind of thing you'd use for an eating challenge or something…
BEELZEBUB
'Tis normal for a demon. We often use this to wrap up a night of drinking.
AZUSA
I'm not a demon, though. But…fine. Maybe I can manage… First, I'll take the noodles beneath the mountain of vegetables and flip it all around, then start eating the noodles first… I know I can eat the veggies even if I'm pretty full. It'll get more difficult if the noodles absorb the broth, so I have to be careful.
BEELZEBUB
You are approaching this quite strategically for a first-timer.
AZUSA
It's pretty popular in all kinds of places, so… I'm kind of familiar.

* * *

Azusa continues to eat her ra-ment.

AZUSA
Yes, I managed to finish it! This is my first ramen in three hundred years, so I guess it was worth it to have two bowls.
FALFA
Wow, Mommy! You ate the whole thing!
SHALSHA
Mom might still be growing. Still evolving at three hundred.
AZUSA
Shalsha, that compliment sounds like it's meant for a middle-aged woman, so please don't say that too much… Phew, I'm so satisfied! Thank you every—
HALKARA
Miss Laika, she's finished the second bowl!
LAIKA
Understood! I will bring out the next one!
AZUSA
What…? Wait, there's more…? I feel like I'm facing off against a boss with two final forms…
BEELZEBUB
For your third bowl, I have chosen my personal favorite type of ra-ment.
AZUSA
Oh no. I have a bad feeling about this.
LAIKA
Here is your extra-spicy ra-ment, Lady Azusa!
AZUSA
Whoa, whoa, whoa! This thing is redder than the flames of hell!

BEELZEBUB

'Tis your own fault.

AZUSA

Huh? What are you talking about?

BEELZEBUB

Anyone can handle a one or two, but you decided to go for a ten.

AZUSA

Wait. I don't remember anyone asking me—

FALFA

Falfa asked you what number you wanted from one to ten.

AZUSA

That's what the number was about?! So it wasn't a personality test; it was a spiciness endurance test!

SHALSHA

A ten is apparently absurdly spicy. You are an exceptional person to take on the challenge, Mom. Still evolving at three hundred.

AZUSA

Do you…like that expression, Shalsha…? *Cough, cough.* Now that it's closer to my face, my eyes are tearing up…

HALKARA

Tears of joy, right? I'm so glad I was able to repay you!

AZUSA

That's quite an optimistic read of the situation. I'm crying because of the spice!

BEELZEBUB

…But there is deep flavor within the spice.

AZUSA

Yeah, it's good. But…I don't think I can handle this as my third bowl.

BEELZEBUB

Then I suppose we shall cancel the rest of the bowls.

AZUSA

Why don't we all just eat together? Let's make this a ramen party!

BEELZEBUB

'Tis ra-ment.

AZUSA

...Okay. I'll go along with you. We'll call it a ra-ment party. Eat up, everyone...

BEELZEBUB – NARRATION

And so everyone enjoyed their own bowls of ra-ment.

FALFA

Wow, it's tasty! Super tasty! Falfa likes this a lot!

SHALSHA

Ra-ment is like philosophy. There are endless possibilities within this bowl.

LAIKA

Yes, the sixth bowl, the rich pork bone ra-ment, was very good. I wish to have a seventh, but may I?

HALKARA

Are you sure you're not eating too much, Miss Laika? But goodness, this *would* be the perfect way to end a night of drinking, wouldn't it?

AZUSA

I'll bring you your next portion then, Laika. Hold on a sec.

SCENE 7

Azusa goes to the kitchen, where Beelzebub is.

AZUSA
Beelzebub, Laika said she's having another bowl.
BEELZEBUB
I see, I see. We've managed to get through all the food after all.
AZUSA
Well, dragons *do* eat a lot… Still, you managed to do something nice for me yet again.
BEELZEBUB
'Twas nothing. Everyone is having a good time. We should do this more often.
AZUSA
Yeah, I guess so.
BEELZEBUB
And, oh. I do want to see you…um…happy…
AZUSA
Beelzebub, are you blushing?
BEELZEBUB
No! Do not say it out loud!
AZUSA
Sorry, sorry. But really, thank you.
BEELZEBUB
Aye. And I wish to see the girls' smiling faces, too.
AZUSA
Hold on. Whose girls are you talking about?
BEELZEBUB
Falfa and Shalsha are so cute. I never tire of seeing them!

AZUSA
I'm never going to let you adopt them, all right?! They're *my* girls! Don't get the wrong idea!
BEELZEBUB
Yes, yes, I know. But...all these big pots lined up in a row is quite a sight, no?
AZUSA
You've gotta boil the pork and chicken bones to make ra-ment. You need big pots like this.
BEELZEBUB
Still, 'tis almost as though...you know.
AZUSA
What?
BEELZEBUB
You know. A witch's house.
AZUSA
Wait. This *is* a witch's house! A literal witch's house! What kind of house did you think you were barging into?!
BEELZEBUB
My girls' house.
AZUSA
Stop calling them that!

BEELZEBUB – NARRATION
And so making ra-ment proved to be a huge success. All because of me, the great demon Beelzebub!

AZUSA – NARRATION
Mm-hmm. It was worth walking so much to work up an appetite. It's not half bad having everyone celebrate me now and again.

The End

Afterword

Hello, this is Kisetsu Morita.

We have a little more info on the anime now! It'll be airing in the spring of 2021. I hope you're as excited as I am! The anime production company will be taking care of everything while I chip away at the novels in the long term, so I hope you continue to enjoy the series!

I have yet another piece of news about the anime. Kaede Hondo, who plays Laika, and Sayaka Senbongi, who plays Falfa, will be starting a little radio show! It will be called *I've Been Killing Slimes for 300 Minutes and Wound Up Talking the Whole Time*!

This information will be released on the official social media and whatnot soon, so please keep an eye out!

Next, some things about the manga.

Last month, the seventh volume of the manga adaptation by Yusuke Shiba, and the third volume of *I was a Bottom-Tier Bureaucrat for 1,500 Years* by Meishi Murakami came out!

Thanks to all your support, the first volume of the manga has gone through fourteen printings. Thank you all so much!

The eighth volume of the manga will be out next March! Please look forward to it!

Also, all the stories from the *I was a Bottom-Tier Bureaucrat for*

1,500 Years spinoff are now in manga form, plus a few manga-only original stories, so it is now complete. And I've already seen the rough storyboards for the next spinoff, *Red-Dragon Academy for Girls*.

No release date has been set yet, but I believe it will be soon. I hope you check it out as well!

Now, a few words about the drama CDs.

Yukari Tamura, who plays Pecora, will be making her first appearance in the next drama CD!

I may have mentioned this before, but when I was sitting in on the recording, I thought to myself, *Oh wow, Pecora's right there*. It really feels like Pecora is speaking. I hope you are able to listen.

And one more thing about the drama CD—as a bonus for this volume, the scripts for the first and second drama CDs have been included in the back (a portion has been edited slightly so that it's easier to read).

Drama CDs generally can't be reprinted, and we heard a lot of feedback that many people have been unable to get their hands on them, especially the very first one, which sold out quickly. As the creator, I want everyone to have access to the content, but it isn't like I can burn these CDs at my own discretion, and I can't exactly sell the special editions with the CD to people who have already bought the regular edition of the novel. All this made for a rather serious problem.

Our compromise was to include the scripts of the drama CDs as part of the novel. Of course, you won't get to hear the voices, but please try to imagine them in your head!

Also, for those who managed to get the drama CDs, please enjoy reading it in print! We also have Benio-sensei's illustrations to go along with the stories, so please be sure to look at those, too!

And finally, some thanks.

Benio, thank you so much for providing us with wonderful illustrations once again! We've been with some of these characters all the way since the very beginning, and I feel safe leaving them in your capable hands.

Thank you so much to Yusuke Shiba and Meishi Murakami, who are in charge of the manga adaptations! Special thanks to Meishi Murakami for sticking around for such a long time! Beelzebub, Vania, and Fatla were so lively by the end, as if they were your own characters. It was a lot of fun to compare and contrast your Beelzebub and Mr. Shiba's Beelzebub.

Thank you to everyone involved with the production of the anime. I know this may seem obvious, but once the anime got started, more people than ever before became involved with the series. I just know it's going to turn out great!

And of course, I offer my genuine gratitude to the readers who picked up this book and all of those who have continued to support the *Killing Slimes* series! I hope to keep developing stories just as fun as the anime, and I hope for your continued support!

The next volume, 15, will be out in January! See you next year!

Kisetsu Morita